T0102871

Whispering Down the Well

From the Writing Group O's Own

Order this book online at www.trafford.com
or email orders@trafford.com
Most Trafford titles are also available at major online book retailers.

© Copyright 2009 O's Own Okanagan Writers' Network.

All rights reserved. No part of this publication may be reproduced, stored in a retrieval system, or
transmitted, in any form or by any means, electronic, mechanical, photocopying, recording, or
otherwise, without the written prior permission of the author.

ISBN: 978-1-4269-2092-9

*Our mission is to efficiently provide the world's finest, most comprehensive book publishing
service, enabling every author to experience success. To find out how to publish your
book, your way, and have it available worldwide, visit us online at www.trafford.com*

Trafford rev. 12/09/2009

 www.trafford.com

North America & international
toll-free: 1 888 232 4444 (USA & Canada)
phone: 250 383 6864 ♦ fax: 812 355 4082

Acknowledgements

We wish to thank the following people who helped us with our writing and with this anthology: Adam Lewis Schroeder and Catherine Mamo for their writing courses which they brought to Osoyoos for us from Okanagan University College. Their feedback helped to bring our stories alive; their rules for critiquing continue to shape our regular meetings.

Carollyne Sinclaire, a relative newcomer to Osoyoos and to O's Own Writers, lent a fresh pair of eyes and her wealth of experience in helping to edit the submissions.

Jack Whittaker works behind the scenes for us in all things technical. Thank you for dedicating your precious free time to our cause. Most of us would be lost in the mire without your expertise.

Our thanks to the Osoyoos and District Arts Council for their Member Grant which assisted the O's Own Writers in publishing *Whispering Down the Well.*

Introduction

Whispering Down the Well grew out of the wish for the O's Own Writers to write about the lives of women, real and imaginary. Women's contributions to society, perhaps because of their nature, have been largely overlooked in previous times; their stories may just as well have been "whispered down the well" for all the notice they garnered.

The main thrust of this collection of poetry and prose is to encourage readers to enjoy the stories of women: their struggles, their victories, their heartaches, their joy. Laugh with them, cry with them, and we hope, appreciate their grit and determination.

These women's ability to make it through the tough times, their unique way of seeing the world, facing challenges and celebrating life may inspire others to view their own lives, or those of loved ones, as worthy of mention.

Although none of us can be assured fifteen minutes of fame, most of us have a story to tell, an experience that marks us for life, sets us apart, turns our life around, opens our eyes to possibilities or puts an end to innocence.

These are our stories.

Contents

Skating Home for Christmas

By Sue Whittaker

When Hope was six years old, she lived on a tugboat all one summer. Her father was a tugboat operator and the tug was the only place they had to live for awhile. The tugboat hauled large booms of logs down the Columbia River to a sawmill, then back it went, up the river, to get another load.

It was Hope's mother's job to keep her five children from drowning, which she did by teaching them how to swim. Hope and her brothers spent more of that summer in the water than out. They learned how to dive off anything and they became quite the little log burlers.

Hope grew to love and respect the river. She learned to avoid rapids after she was pulled under by swirling water once. It seemed like ages before she was spat back out. And some sections of the river ran through narrow sections so fast that you made sure you were on the tug in those places.

When Hope grew up she became a teacher. In 1923, she was teaching in Deer Park, a tiny settlement on the banks of the Columbia River. Her family lived about twenty miles down the river in a bigger town called Castlegar. As Christmas approached she planned to travel home on the SS Minto, a sternwheeler. But the weather turned so cold that the river froze solid from bank to bank. What was she to do? There was no road out of Deer Park and no trail to ride a horse. Everybody traveled downriver by boat.

After giving the problem a lot of thought, Hope decided to skate the twenty miles to Castlegar.

She was able to borrow a pair of hand-forged metal blades which strapped to her winter boots by way of rough pieces of leather with crude metal buckles attached. She was up very early on the day after school let out. Flashing a brave smile, she chatted with her landlady's kids who accompanied her to the river's edge to say good-bye and hold her knapsack containing one jam sandwich and an apple. She buckled on her skates, wrapped her scarf around her face, pulled on her mittens and found her footing on the thick ice.

"Here'th your knapthack, Mith McGauley," lisped the youngest child, handing it over to her.

"Good Luck!" called the others as she pushed off.

"Let's hope there's a thaw so you don't have to skate upriver to get back," the oldest boy joked.

"Keep your fingers crossed . . . and thanks for the skates and all your help." she called back. "Merry Christmas!"

The sun had not yet risen when they said goodbye, the children following her progress until the turn in the river. With one last wave, she rounded the bend and started east towards Castlegar. The wind was at her back and she set a brisk pace . . . push, glide, push, glide, push, glide. The ice was very smooth. She leaned her body forward, drew every ounce of forward momentum she could from her arms and flew down river, released from the cares of a one-room school teacher and eager to see her family as soon as possible.

She welcomed the first actual rays of sunlight that flowed over her right shoulder and cast long winter shadows across the ice. Now she had small benchmarks on which she could focus, "I'll slow down a bit between the shadow of that big ponderosa pine and that rock outcropping up on my right." "I'll see if I can skate with my hands behind my back until I get to that sunny patch up ahead." As small goals were achieved, she felt less fear and more of a sense of adventure.

She was not entirely alone on her journey down the frozen expanse. Occasionally she noted eagles soaring above, some even landing on the ice to strut about indignantly as they investigated this frozen barrier between them and their breakfast. Deer had moved down to the valley bottom in response to the severe winter conditions. At intervals, she glimpsed several small herds by the river's edge, curiously attracted to the swishing of her skates. Cougars were a worry for her but if they noted her passing they gave no chase and she was blissfully unaware of their presence.

Most of her tension came from the rumbling noises arising from the ice. She had been told that the groaning and cracking came as a result of the water level dropping below the ice after it froze. But it was one thing to know this intellectually, and quite another to convince herself that some huge crack was not likely to open up in front of her, or even worse, beneath her. As much as she loved water, she didn't want to die alone and unnoticed beneath the river ice, to be swept downstream and then disgorged into the ocean to become fish food.

Forcing herself to consider more cheerful thoughts, she conjured up a picture of her three tiny brothers, the last of eleven children. Hope's main reason for going home was to give her mother a rest over the holiday and bring some Christmas cheer to her poor family. She had been able to save enough money from her tiny salary to buy each little boy a pair of winter boots enabling the children to venture outside to play. Plans were afoot to cut down several old, donated, adult jackets and make parkas for the kids. She hoped there would be something left from her paycheck to be able to slip at least one toy under the tree for each child. At present, their only diversion was a half-grown cat that could surely use a break from the rough attentions of three small children.

Looking up to her left she noticed the bobbing light of a kerosene lantern heading toward a small outhouse sheltered in the trees edging a little farm she was passing. Some one didn't like spiders, she guessed.

A rooster crowed and a horse made it known that breakfast would be a good idea. This reassuring human presence lifted her spirits and put new energy in her stroke. In an especially glassy section of ice she decided, what the heck! She spun around in a couple of loops, practiced her backwards strokes for a short distance and imagined she had music and a partner. Dancing on ice! Now wouldn't that be a sight to see!

As the porridge she had eaten for breakfast left her to the mercy of her growling stomach, she stopped at what she estimated to be the halfway point in her journey. She retrieved half a sandwich from her knapsack and decided to put the rest of her lunch inside her coat. It was almost frozen. While she ate, leaning up against an ancient fallen tree at the edge of the river, she worked at dislodging the heavy border of ice and snow that rimmed the hem of her long woolen skirt. As much as she hoped it gave her outfit a snow princess look, the weight of the ice was considerable. She knew the last half of her trip would be the most difficult as she grew tired and her skates lost the edge that her landlady's oldest son had put on them the night before. Off she started again, thankful for the lighter skirt but wishing she had something to shield her eyes from the now bright sun and the blinding reflection from the surrounding banks of snow. She found that if she pulled her scarf up in one layer over her eyes she could still see enough to carry on and the relief from the glare was very welcome.

Bundled up to her eyebrows she heard rather than saw the children she was approaching two hours later. Pulling her scarf down to her nose, she slowed as she saw them coming to meet her.

"Hi," she called. "Are you children from Robson?"

They assured her they were, and asked if she had come to join their game of hockey. When she told them she had just skated from Deer Park, one little fellow, with eyes as big as saucers said, "My mom would whup me if I skated to Deer Park."

Knowing she was within a few miles of Castlegar, Hope ate the last of her lunch and set a more leisurely pace. She had things to do when she got to town. No point in wearing herself out before she got there.

She wondered if there was anybody new in town. Anybody her age who might show up at the New Year's party and want to dance. And maybe she could organize a toboggan party over the holiday. They certainly had the snow for it.

With the railway bridge that led to Castlegar in sight, Hope began looking for an easy place to leave the river and climb to the small road above. Choosing her route, she sat on a boulder at the edge of the river and removed her blades, stuffing them in her knapsack.

Her legs were very wobbly as she started up the embankment. Looking up she saw a young man looking down at her.

"Hello," he greeted her. "Where have you come from? I've been watching your progress down the river."

She told him about the predicament she had been in with the river freezing and the Minto unable to sail. "So I borrowed some skates, and here I am," she said, laughing. "And I'm very glad to be here too. I'm Hope."

"I'm sure you are," he replied. "I'm Ross. Glad to meet you."

He held out his hand and pulled her up the last few steps to the road. They walked in to Castlegar together. Hope caught up on the latest news in town, only parting from Ross to enter the general store to see if she could find those snow boots for her brothers.

Well, that put a hole in a twenty dollar bill, she thought, as she left the store. But she had the boots, a spinning top, a book of nursery rhymes and a toy train for her brothers. For her mother she had stockings and a new dress that she thought was too good a deal to pass up, and for her father, warm gloves. That left only enough money for yarn for a sweater that she would knit before the New Year's party the whole community attended. You never knew who might be there, she thought. Things appeared to be looking up in Castlegar. She might have somebody besides her older brother to dance with this year.

She stomped on to the family's front porch, her tired arms sore from carrying her purchases and her legs ready to give out. But it was all worth it when her little brothers burst out the door and wrapped themselves around her legs in a noisy welcome. She looked up into her mother's tired and worn face, surprise masking the worst of her troubles.

"Hope, how did you get here, pray tell?" Tears glistened in her eyes.

"Let me get in and warm my feet, and I'll tell you how I skated home for Christmas."

A Full Life

By Sue Whittaker

A mother and father,
sisters and brothers,
grandparents who left us too soon
but friendships which lasted for life.

Teachers who mentored,
colleagues who gave of themselves,
and daughters who arrived
when we needed them most.

We, the two of us, husband and wife,
Dad and Mom,
rich in love
and privileged to live a full life.

This Day's Challenge

By Maureen Kresfelder

My day was full,
happily so,
walking and talking
with my spouse
along the lake shore.
Then lunching with friends
who are gourmets
as well as opera buffs
and sharing with them
La Traviata, a tour de force
of great love and tragic death,
sung out and acted
by a lusty Russian soprano
and a sensual Latin tenor.
Then home, not to romance my husband
though it had occurred to me,
but rather to finish writing a review
of *A Thousand Splendid Suns*
and then forgetting
to tell whence that poetic
title came.
And next, talking to my mother
and to my delight
hearing an almost happy note
in her tone and disposition.
At last, settling in with my neglected spouse
with a glass of wine and cheese and crackers
to watch a commercial free broadcast
of Dr. Martin, whose surly behaviour

we love to disparage, and a nature program
whose animal violence should be x-rated.
And afterwards, back to the computer
to pick up this day's challenge
to write this poem.

Queen of the Pond

By Jody Chadderton

Miss Lulubelle was the luckiest duck
on Peanut Pond.
Only she's not a duck,
she's a majestic white domestic goose
like Mother Goose.
Also, she's not "Miss Lulu" after all.
Turns out she's "Mr. Louis."
But the sex change
comes much later in the story.

Lulu moved to Peanut Pond
in Osoyoos a year and a half ago.
Where was I?
I walk past Peanut Pond
at least six times every week,
but I didn't know
someone had a pet goose
until last fall.

That's when we started painting
a home on the Pond
and we heard "Lulu, Lulu, Lulu. . ."
over and over,
over and over.
Someone's kid or dog or cat? we wondered.
Wrong. Finally Lulu swam home,
Lulu the goose.

Six times a week at least
I walk past Peanut Pond.
Now I look for Miss Lulubelle
every single time.

I listen for the incessant
Honk-onk, Honk-onk
as opposed to the usual
Quack quack quack
Quack quack quack of the mallards,
or whatever sounds
the Canada geese make.
Honk-onk, Honk-onk too, perhaps.

I admit I'm musically-challenged.
I know I can't tell the difference
in bird-song
between a chirp and a tweet.
Maybe a birder can tell me
the difference
between Canada goose Honk!
and Lulu-speak Honk!

Ever since I discovered
Miss Lulubelle, queen of Peanut Pond,
I have been
singing her praises.
I love that majestic white goose.
I tell two friends
and they tell two friends
and so on, and so on . . .

Then suddenly Lulu makes the news
with the headline,
"Lulu's goose not cooked, yet,"
(Osoyoos Times, March 19/08.)
A silly play on words.

So if I may be corny in response,
let me say that
we, the people of Peanut Pond,
get along swimmingly with the fauna.
Except, of course,
for some spoilsport
who thinks that Honk-onk
sounds worse than:
Quack, quack, quack
and whatever the Canada geese say.

Shame on you,
you Lulu-hater,
shame on you
for bringing the story
to the fore
and for outing my beloved
Miss Lulubelle.
Now she is Louis.
The newspaper says so.
But Miss Lulubelle, always, to me.

Dance Shoes

By Maureen Olson

Time to spring clean, so I started in my clothes closet. Inside the first box I opened were a pair of dainty silver dancing shoes. The toe is open, a slender strap formed the sling and the heel is higher than I wear now. I had to try them on! How did I ever dance in these narrow, fragile-looking shoes? I could hardly get my foot inside and as for standing on these heels, not anymore. I now wear low heels and a B width. In fact I can't remember the last time I wore these beautiful shoes. I put them in a box for the Thrift Shop.

Later in the day memories came flooding back, not of the last time I wore them but of the first time. Alan had asked me to go to a special dance to be held at the Commodore Ballroom in Vancouver. It promised to be quite an event. My pink crystallette dress, empire style with a full skirt, needed just the right pair of shoes. These I found after trying on numerous pairs: high heels, moderate heels, narrow and enclosed, or straps. I decided this pair was the most comfortable, a necessity as I knew how much Alan enjoyed jiving.

This dance would be so much fun. Great music, drinks (in a brown paper bag under the table), good friends. The floor at the Commodore was special: it was sprung with horsehair so when there was jiving, it felt like the floor was dancing too. The climb up the narrow stairs from the sidewalk to the dance floor added to the excitement. The swing door revealed a large room, dimly lit, with tables covered with white cloths along both sides, highlighted by the stage holding the twelve-piece band. The central chandelier was spectacular, adding to the magic of this venue. A venue used by University of British Columbia student bodies for the faculty fundraising dances which were always sold out.

We greeted our friends and sat for a moment to listen to the band which started to play *Great Balls of Fire.* Neither of us could sit still; we got up to jive. We danced through two sets of music then went to the table to rest and to dance with our friends. Then Alan and I stepped up again. Over and under, around behind, in and out, spins, barrel roll, step back, two forward. The band kept playing, and we kept jiving. Gradually, I became aware there was more room for us to move. We danced harder. I heard clapping and someone calling, "Go, Alan, Go!" The band played faster, we danced faster and the crowd grew. Finally the band stopped. We held hands as we walked back to the table, a chance to catch our breath and cool off. After a short break we took a turn dancing with our friends and then danced together again.

The next time we stopped, a short time later, a young man came up to Alan to say, "You did it, we timed you, twenty minutes! None of us thought you'd be able to do that!" I looked at Alan wondering if he knew he was being timed. He looked at me sheepishly. What an amazing evening!

Farewell dance shoes. Thanks for awakening the memory.

The Shower

By Anita L. Trapler

A dark eyed child
with tanned and glowing skin,
quickly lathered tiny arms, her tiny legs
and feet.

Pearly bubbles gathered on the tiled floor,
till she inclined her wee face and stooped
to see
all the tiny pearls swish away.

Indomitable Woman

By Anita L. Trapler

Antonia and Johann lived and worked on a small acreage within striking distance of Lodz, Poland. Lodz was the second largest city after Warsaw. From the earliest nineteenth century, Lodz was famous for its textiles. Almost half of the city's population was Polish Jews. Many Polish people were employed by Jewish factory owners and entrepreneurs to weave cloth and sew clothing. Antonia and Johann preferred the rural life.

Life on the farm was hard for Antonia and Johann, but predictable and peaceful. And then in September, 1939, the Germans invaded Poland. No more could they expect peace or predictability. Their country was now ruled by a foreign power.

A month or so after the annexation of her beloved Poland, Antonia cycled her reliable heavy-framed bicycle into Lodz. Just as she entered the city, Antonia swerved to avoid a speeding jeep driven by a Nazi. She lost control, flew over the handle bars and landed in a stony ditch. Almost all of her front teeth were chipped or broken. Now there was no choice but to continue on to Lodz; she needed a dentist.

Lodz was no longer the beautiful city she knew. She was painfully aware of the changes she saw. The Germans were everywhere in the city streets. So many "Heil Hitlers." So many burned out businesses. And, to her horror, so many corpses hanging from the lampposts. She also witnessed a pair of German officers restraining an elderly rabbi while one of them sliced off his beard and cut his hair. Antonia averted her eyes and kept silent. She had not known such fear until Hitler's rule. Her city errands completed, she hastened to return to the sanctuary of her farm and her family.

She and Johann had been trying to make a living on five acres of land. The original land had been carved up several times for inheritance purposes. Antonia worked ceaselessly to grow a vegetable garden and raise a few cows and chickens. She sold or traded the surplus vegetables, meat, eggs and milk. Her arduous labours were visible in her work-worn callused hands. "It was worth it," she said, "because I feed my family."

Whenever Johann could find employment he worked as a carpenter. He was hired by the "Bautruppen" — a work crew for the Germans camped outside of Lodz. The men built barns and houses and did repair jobs to public and private buildings. Only German was spoken, only German permitted.

Hundreds of years of Polish blood coursed through Antonia's veins. There was even some nobility in the family tree and a good ability to "think-for–oneself." She more than once told me, "By Hitler's time, some German women saw I had just one son. They told me I should make more babies for the Reich. Yah, I thought and who would feed them?" Women, who birthed lots of babies during the Third Reich, were given medals.

World War II squeezed all the Polish people like pulp, with the German army on one side and the Russian army on the other. Word spread: "The Russians are coming."

Antonia understood that if the Russians found out that Johann was of German heritage, he would either be hanged or shot on the spot. At the very least, he would be sent to a gulag in Siberia. Antonia hid all their personal documents inside a wall of the farmhouse including birth certificates, baptismal certificates and anything else that could identify them.

In 1940, when the Russian troops could be seen in the distant fields, their son, Hans, now twelve years old, leapt out of a window and fled ahead of his parents. He and his parents were not reunited for over a year.

Johann and Antonia, too, fled on foot. But the Russians overtook them and they soon found themselves in a Russian camp. These Russians were on the way to crush the Germans. Johann passed himself off as Polish. One of the Russians noticed Johann's hard and callused hands and asked him what he did for a living. Johann replied in Polish, "I am a carpenter."

The Russians were gleeful because they needed carpenters to build crates for the appropriated furniture, art work, carpets and other valuables, destined for Russia as reparations. Johann was given a number of Polish men to work under his direction. Antonia cautioned him, "You treat these people well. If they find out you are German, they will tear you to pieces."

The Russian Commissars were multilingual and many of these were Jews who also spoke German among other languages. Nearly all the Russian men were heavy 100 Proof vodka drinkers. One night, Johann was invited to join a party of forty to fifty men. The more Johann drank this powerful vodka, the more knowledgeable he seemed. In Russian, he mightily praised Stalin and all the good work he was doing for the people. He praised communism and sang about Stalin in the loudest voice he could muster.

The next morning, there was a sharp knock on the door. One of the Russian officers wished to speak to Johann right away. The chief Commissar had been impressed with his enthusiasm for communism. He hoped to enlist him to work for the Russian bureaucracy.

Seriously hung over, Johann could barely walk. So it was that Antonia went in his place to report to this Russian officer. He had a deep, white scar running from his eye to his chin. The more Antonia talked, the more livid his face became. In Russian she said, "My husband got very, very drunk last night. He knows nothing about Stalin or this war. He's a carpenter. He gets crazy when he drinks. He doesn't know what he's talking about." The Russian officer raised his hand and told her to get out. However, there were no repercussions, much to the relief of both Johann and Antonia.

A few days later, a Russian Jew, who had been travelling with the Russian soldiers, approached Johann and Antonia. He said to Johann, "You're not Polish. I can hear that by your speech and your accent." He turned and left. Both of them were terrified he would betray them. But this Jewish man said nothing about either of them to anyone that they were aware of.

As the fighting between the Germans and the Russians became fiercer, the Russian camp fell into disarray; Antonia and Johann slipped away unnoticed. At the time they left camp Antonia was already 7 months pregnant with her second child. Her ankles had become swollen during this pregnancy; at times, she was unable to walk. Fortunately, Johann salvaged a child's wagon from a ditch. The wagon was sturdy, made from wood, with thick rubber wheels. With that wagon, he pulled Antonia when her legs would not support her. Antonia was only thirty-three years old, but she resembled a woman long past her childbearing years.

Eventually, Johann and Antonia found their way to the city of Gera, in East Germany. The war had barely ended when the Russians occupied East Germany. Many people, like themselves, were trapped behind Communist lines. Antonia gave birth to a son, Dietrich, who barely weighed three pounds. She vowed silently that this child would live, that he would thrive; that he would get an education and God-willing, grow up in a democracy. Even then Antonia and Johann were planning their escape to freedom.

Food was rationed for a long time after the war. It was mostly women who stood for hours in lengthy lineups with coupons for an egg or a ration of potatoes. Women like Antonia, with babies or young children, would receive an extra ration once or twice a week.

While Antonia stood in a lineup one morning, she heard a woman cry out, "Stalin, where is the soap? We need soap to get clean." A couple of policemen walked towards her then each grasped one of her arms. The struggling woman was taken away, never to be seen again.

When an election was called in East Germany, everyone had to vote. I asked Antonia, "Who did you vote for?" Her eyes widened in surprise, "Why Stalin, of course." Communists circulated in the voting hall to supervise the election and ensure everyone voted the right way.

There was a lot of work in East Germany for both men and single women. If you were unemployed, you were instantly rounded up to be questioned by the police. If you were deemed a shirker, you could be sent to a work camp in Siberia. Antonia and Johann were always busy. Just surviving took all their energy and time.

Stalin encouraged people to raise rabbits for food. Johann did. But he had to steal grasses and clover to feed these animals. If he had been caught, he could have been jailed or sent to a work camp or even shot.

In East Germany, Antonia and Johann were eventually reunited with their elder son, Hans. Antonia said she never gave up hope that they would find him. She just knew "in her bones" that he was still alive and looking for them. Johann spent many days searching for his lost son. By bicycle he traveled all over devastated Germany before the borders between East and West Germany had been established. He finally found his son's name on a Red Cross list in southern Germany. He had been working as an apprentice jeweler in the Sudetenland.

When an opportunity came to escape East Germany, Antonia and Johann seized it. With the help of courageous friends, they headed for a better world with their children. They first escaped across the border to West Germany. From there they flew to Montreal, Canada. Their arrival in Canada in 1951 was one of the happiest days of their lives. They were free, at last.

When Antonia, Johann and their two sons arrived in Canada, they came with nothing more than the clothing on their backs, fifty dollars and some tanned rabbit skins. They temporarily lived with relatives who sponsored them. Their relative's house was already filled with children and adults so there was no room at the inn. Johann, Antonia, and their children were compelled to sleep in a vacant chicken coop. But the walls were whitewashed and the rooms immaculate. In winter, downy, feathered bedding kept them warm. They were just glad and thankful they had a safe and welcoming place to live.

No one in Antonia and Johann's family could speak any English. However, German mixed with Yiddish, Ukrainian, Russian, and the Polish language had served them well in the Europe of World War II, and these languages would prove to be helpful in Canada as well.

Antonia found work in a hotel laundry where her fellow workers spoke Polish, Russian, Ukrainian with a little German and Yiddish tossed in. So for the first few years, English was very difficult for her to learn. But learn to speak English, she did. However broken her English was in this adopted land, Antonia fought to make herself understood.

Johann worked all his life as a carpenter in Canada. He was a perfectionist and really took ownership of his work. He'd started out at the age of twelve building wagon wheels. Because of his expert craftsmanship he was much in demand for work in his new country too. And after a little while, through hard work and thrift, Antonia, Johann and their two sons had a real house to call home.

In Poland, Johann only completed a grade two education while Antonia completed grade four. Both of them had to leave school early to work and help support their families. Many years later, at home in her kitchen in Canada, Antonia often sighed, "Maybe, I was lucky to have no high school education. During the War, so many people with higher education were rounded up and shot." Then, she would shrug and return to washing the dishes.

But Antonia and Johann did make sure that their sons had the educational opportunities they never did. Both Hans and

Dietrich completed high school and went on to pursue university educations.

Antonia, in her senior years, kept a meticulous, showpiece flower garden. Her red, white and pink rhododendrons and other varieties of flowers rivaled those of Butchart Gardens. She had created her own vision of heaven in her backyard. With the luxury of leisure time and money, she grew snowdrops in January, crocuses in February along with daffodils and tulips — in fact, her garden held colour and promise 12 months of the year. But calluses, broken finger nails and splinters were a thing of the past. She took pride in her soft hands and smiling, would occasionally hold them up for me to admire.

After Johann died at the age of seventy-seven, Antonia did not learn to drive. Instead she walked everywhere and bused back home. She maintained her garden well into her 80's. I marveled at Antonia's stamina. Until she died at 93, she remained the proud matriarch of the family.

This indomitable woman was my mother-in-law.

The Deadly Spitfire

By Sally Swedberg

I was in our kitchen preparing lunch on a sultry, quiet Sunday afternoon in March. Our family had arrived home about a half hour before from the church service held at the Liberian High School chapel. Paul, my Chaplain husband, had preached the morning sermon.

The rainy season usually began in April in Liberia, West Africa, where we were serving as missionaries. But there had been a torrential downpour the night before, causing the high humidity. The small electric fan with its whirring burr, the joyous sounds of our boys playing and the clinking of dishes as I set the table were the only sounds that broke the silence.

Our four sons, home for a four day weekend, from Thursday until Sunday, would be going back to the missionary school today. Paul would be driving them the fifty miles to school later on in the afternoon. In the meantime, the boys were enjoying playing Frisbee in our spacious backyard with a background of jungle. Paul was relaxing with a book on our large screened-in porch overlooking the yard. I thought to myself, how good it is to have the boys home, having fun together, and being able to go to church as a family.

Suddenly, from outside, Eric's panic-stricken voice broke through my reverie, shattering the tranquility of the afternoon. "Help me! Somebody, help me! It's a cobra!"

I was taken by surprise with my heart skipping a beat. I had thought our 11-year-old son, Eric, was happily playing with his brothers, 14-year-old Dan, 9-year-old Philip and 7-year-old Michael. Had they all gone too close to the jungle and met up with a cobra? Were they all in danger? One question after another raced through my mind as I dropped the dish towel on the floor and ran towards the back door.

No, no, that can't be it, I thought, Eric's voice sounded too close to the house. I almost bumped into Eric as he stumbled into the kitchen, holding his hands over one eye. Dan, Philip and Michael followed close behind him. At that moment, Paul came running from the porch.

Eric fell to his knees pitifully crying out, "Mom, Dad, the cobra spit in my eye and I can't see anything!"

Paul and I knew what this could mean. It was typical of cobras to aim for a person's eye, when disturbed. The poison from their venom can cause permanent blindness unless treated right away. We had heard about a Liberian man who had experienced that fate.

I began silently praying and reassuring Eric with my hands upon his shoulders. "Dad and I are here, honey. Everything will be just fine." This seemed to comfort him a bit but his crying continued. Paul, who was always so capable in emergencies, knew just what to do to help Eric. How thankful I was that he was home and not out in one of the villages, on an evangelistic bush trip. I was sure that God was already answering my unspoken prayers.

Dan wanted to know how he could help Eric. Philip and Michael looked on with frightened and bewildered faces. I knew they needed to be distracted, so I gathered up the mangoes I had prepared for them to eat and took them to their room to play for awhile. They seemed anxious to be away from the terrifying scene.

"Come with me, Eric. Like your mom says, everything is going to be alright." Paul put his arms underneath Eric's arms and gently lifted him to his feet. He guided him into the bathroom. "You come along too, Dan, I'll find a way for you to help. Do you have any pain in your eye, Eric?"

Between gulping sobs, he answered, "Yeah Dad, it's stinging a lot and everything looks grey and blurry."

"Okay now Eric, here's what I'm going to do. I'm going to wash your eye out with lots of warm water. It won't hurt. In fact, it'll feel good. So just put your head over the sink with your damaged eye turned towards me. Hold your eye open with your fingers. Keep your mouth closed so no water will get in it. Dan, you can hold this hand towel over his good eye."

Paul took a plastic glass by the sink, filled it with warm tap water and began pouring it into Eric's eye to rinse out the venom. The warm water eased the stinging a bit. Eric cooperated as best he could but it was awkward to keep his head twisted to one side.

"Are we almost finished, Dad? My clothes are really getting wet."

Paul threw several bath towels down on the floor and I wasn't sure why he was doing that although Eric seemed to have a better sense about what was going on by then. "It won't be long now, Eric," Paul said. "I'm going to try something different that may work better. Lie down on the floor with these towels under your head while I rinse your eye some more. Dan, you can keep that towel over his good eye. Eric was getting restless, but he gave a sigh and obeyed his dad whom he trusted. Finally, Paul was finished and asked Eric, "Can you see anything out of your eye yet?"

"Not really Dad. It's still blurry and hurting me some." And he started crying again.

As I watched the procedure I prayed silently, Dear God, give Eric and each of us your comfort and peace. And show us what more we should do to save his eye.

Dan helped Eric up from the floor. He looked so pathetic and sad my mother's heart went out to him. I embraced him and kissed his forehead as I said, "Don't worry, honey, I love you and God loves you even more. He's our Great Physician and he will heal your eye. Just you wait and see, okay?" Even as I said this I was scared and trembling inside.

Paul and I knew we had to move quickly. The next step was to take Eric to the hospital which was 15 miles away, on a dirt road, full of potholes. Paul decided we should have Deanna, a nurse, come over and check Eric's eye. She was visiting missionaries from Ghana who lived up the road from us. I called her while Paul changed Eric into some dry clothes.

Deanna came over right away and looked at Eric's eye through a magnifying glass. She noticed a kind of film covering the pupil of his eye.

"You should get him to the hospital right now," she advised. She spoke calmly, trying not to alarm our family. "I think you should leave as soon as possible. Doctor Baum has medication for this condition. Your dad treated your eye the right way, Eric, so you're going to be just fine."

She hoped this was so but she looked unsure. "Maybe Dan could go along and keep washing Eric's eye until you get there," she suggested.

"I was just going to ask if I could do that," said Dan.

"We'd love to have you along, Dan. Let's get started. Mom can pray for us and keep the home fires burning."

We sent them off with plenty of towels and warm water. I lifted up two quick unspoken prayers: Lord, give them a safe trip with no car or road problems. And help them to get there on time to save Eric's eye.

I got lunch for the younger boys and myself after they left. I continued to pray silently and my faith was strengthened and peace settled on my shoulders. I knew Paul would drive our four-wheel drive Peugeot carefully and slowly over the rough roads, as he always did, even though he knew how serious the situation was. There were many accidents on that road because of speeding, so he always took every precaution.

I got the whole story when they got home. Paul told us that Dan showed a lot of maturity for a 14-year-old. He kept bathing

Eric's eye over a pail and made sure that the towels kept him dry. After forty-five minutes on the very rough road, they arrived at Zorzor Lutheran Hospital.

Because Deanna had phoned ahead, alerting the hospital to our arrival, Doctor Baum immediately checked Eric's eye and put some drops of cortisone in it. Eric was nervous but the Doctor's reassuring words calmed him down. He said the stinging was only temporary and in a few minutes it would be gone. The doctor said they did well to get to the hospital so quickly thanks to the quick and skilful actions of everyone.

Paul added, "And we know we were blessed to have God's help. Right boys?"

"Right on, Dad," they all agreed.

Of course we all wanted Eric to tell us how the accident had happened. Eric said, "I wanted to go up to the attic to get one of our old games for us to play, later. When I opened the door leading up to the attic, the cobra was coiled up on the third step. It was level with my eyes as I stood on the step outside. I must have frightened him so he paid me back. Then we were both afraid. I'm sure he was after that scrawny chicken we were given that we tied up under the steps. He must have got in through that hole in the bottom of the door. I'll bet you anything that's what happened, huh Dad?"

"I'm sure that was it, son. How is your eye feeling now? Doctor Baum said you will need to be given those drops two times a day—morning and evening—for ten days. We'll make those arrangements when we take you back to school."

"Yeah, that won't be so bad, huh, Eric?" said Dan. "Can you see our ugly faces yet?" he kidded, giving Eric a playful punch.

"Yeah, I can make out who you are and things are not so blurry as they were," said Eric with a smile.

"That's good, that's good," said Paul. "In your prayers tonight, I'm sure you'll remember to thank your mom for all of her prayers and support. She played a very big part in the outcome of this drama."

"I sure will remember to do that, Dad!" Eric promised, with a big smile for me.

And what more could a mother want?

Pat Takes a Walk

By Allene Halliday

"So, you want to know what the worst crisis of my childhood was? You little guys sure come up with some tough questions for your poor old mom!

"Well, let's see. I guess it would have to be when your Aunt Pat, who was only three years old at the time, got bored one day. Of course, the one who really got the brunt of this crisis was your grandmom.

"We lived in Hayward then—on Main Street. When it happened, your Aunt Elaine and I were about three blocks away in school. It was old Edwin Markham's Elementary School right in the centre of town. Pat had to have walked right by it but neither of us saw her.

"It happened like this, best I can understand, since I wasn't right there when she decided to do this crazy thing. Anyway, your aunt was playing in the sandbox in our backyard—or maybe she was on the swing—well, it doesn't matter. She was by herself while Mom was washing clothes on our back porch.

"It was a screened-in porch, so it was like an extra little room. In those days washers only washed; they didn't rinse and they didn't spin the excess water out of the clothes. There was a metal contraption connected to the back. The thing had two rollers and was called a wringer or mangle or something like that. Mom turned a handle on the side of it as she pushed the soaking wet laundry between those rollers. It would get a stranglehold on the wash and wring out most of the sudsy water as Mom pulled everything through before dumping it all into rinse water in the utility sink next to the washer. Then she had to push it all back

29

through this wringer thingy. The wash came out of that mangling machine looking flatter than Kansas. But it was still wet. Since there were no automatic dryers back then, she put everything into a big wicker basket and carried it outside where she hung the laundry on our clothesline to dry.

"Yes, it was a lot of work and it took a lot of time, but you know, Mom always sang while she washed. That's why she didn't notice Pat leaving the backyard. She was busy, the washer was noisy and she was singing. Mom thought my sister was safe and playing happily. After all, that's how she'd been just a few minutes before Mom went outside to hang up the wash and discovered her youngest daughter was gone. What a shock!

"Our yard was fenced with gates on both sides of the house. Pat left by one of those gates and she took our big, old, golden brown dog, Mooch, with her.

"Why would Aunt Pat do that? Well, like I said, she was bored. She didn't have anyone to play with—except old Mooch. And he wasn't the liveliest playmate.

"As you can imagine, Mom was horrified when she couldn't find her little girl in the back or front yard. Worse, she was nowhere in sight.

"What did your grandmom do? She ran to the neighbours, the Whittakers and the Sullivans, on both sides of our house. No, Pat wasn't visiting either of them, but they assured Mom they would watch for her. That wasn't much help. Mom ran up and down our street calling frantically for my sister.

"She couldn't find her anywhere. Finally, she phoned the police. Since I was only in the first grade, I came home earlier than your Aunt Elaine, so I saw Mom getting into the police car. What's happening? ran through my little mind as I raced over to her. She bent down to tell me she had to look for Pat, who had run away or—been kidnapped. She began to cry and said Mrs. Dow would take care of me until she got back.

"Well, that was upsetting. Oh, I liked little, old Mrs. Dow, all right. She was a dear widow lady who came to stay with us whenever Mom needed someone to babysit. Mrs. Dow was like a grandmom to us kids. But I wanted to ride in the police car. I especially wanted to turn on the siren so everybody would look at us as we sped along the streets. But NO! I had to stay home.

"Where did they find Aunt Pat? Would you believe that my little three- year-old sister walked right through the whole downtown of Hayward, past Bret Harte Junior High School, and right up the hill to where the road turned and went out into the country before someone noticed her? She had sat down at the top of the hill because she was hot, tired, thirsty and hungry by then. Old Mooch lay down beside her panting, with his tongue hanging out from all that exertion. They were a sorry sight.

"A woman, Mrs. Preston, came out of her house to get her mail and saw the tiny, exhausted child with the big dog across the road. And she recognized my little sister!

"I wish you'd stop interrupting me so much. Yes, she recognized Pat because Hayward was just a little town in those days. Almost everybody knew everyone else in town. Besides, her own daughter, Joan, was in my class. Mrs. Preston invited your aunt to come into the house for lunch.

"Oh, yes! I'm sure that lady gave poor, tuckered out Mooch some water and a dog biscuit.

"Anyway, while Pat was eating soup, Mrs. Preston called the police. I suppose she tried our house first and Mrs. Dow had told her that Mom was out in the patrol car searching for our two wanderers.

"Did Aunt Pat get a spanking when Mom and the police came to get her? I don't think so. I suppose your grandmom was so relieved by the happy outcome of the whole worrisome ordeal that all she could do was hug and kiss her. After all, Pat hadn't meant to be naughty. She just wanted to visit our Aunt Mil, who lived out in the country. There were cows and chickens and horses to play with at Aunt Mil's. There was a creek full of pollywogs running through the big, grassy fields out back, too.

"No, of course the pollywogs weren't running through the fields. It was the creek with the pollywogs in it that was doing the running. Oh, for heavens sake, would you stop being so pesky? You knew what I meant!

"There were all kinds of pretty wildflowers to pick, especially buttercups, and rainbow-coloured butterflies to chase as they fluttered about. Oh, yes! Aunt Mil's farm was lots more fun than our backyard. No wonder Pat wanted to go there. Who could blame her?

"And she actually was halfway there before Joan's mom saw her. (But, yes, you're right. It certainly was naughty for Pat to leave our backyard without Mom's permission.)

"No, she never did that again. She'd learned her lesson, whether Mom spanked her or not. It had not been much fun trying to walk all that way. The farm was about three miles away, you know. When you stop to think about it though, it was pretty clever of her to know the way, wasn't it? We'd always driven there.

"Would I be as nice as Grandmom was about it, if one of you were to wander off to visit Aunt Pat without permission? Better not put me to the test, boys!"

Remembering Nurse Milli

By Everett J. Marwood

A house of horrors, the boy thought. Not the House of Horrors at the amusement park. He knew that to be a fake, but this was a reality more terrifying than a mere mirage. To his left a contorted body drooped. Across the room sat a pocked and ashen face. A mummified leg pointed towards the boy. Moans and sobs sang out. He thought he heard tears trickle down a cheek. Could one hear tears?

The boy's mother had insisted he stay here in the lobby of the Fifth Street Emergency Medical Clinic while she hastily made off with his ailing sister.

Trembling, he fixated on the darkness of the night, the wind and the rain. The blushing droplets of water that formed on the windows were coloured by the white and red pulsing lights of the emergency medical services van. The glow of the street lamps on the busy doorway projected animated shadows, eerie images that traversed the broken bodies encircling the boy. All the while the clatter of voices, sirens, and the hurried movements numbed him.

"My name is Sears," Milli said, "Nurse Sears, Nurse Milli Sears. No relation to the Sears of retail fame of course. Why do I say that? I could be, I suppose, but I know of no relationship. You can call me Milli. That's my favorite name."

The noise subsided some, the lights mellowed.

The boy became aware that he was being addressed. He looked up, saw her gentle eyes, heard her gentle voice.

"I came from the English countryside, at least my Mom and Dad did, and not yesterday but years ago." The slight lilt that lingered in her voice confirmed her claim. "They suppose they brought me along because at age four, I was too small to stay. They settled us in Rimouski. Work with the government in fisheries took my dad and us there. Rimouski is situated on the shores of the great fleuve Saint Laurent, as it opens up to the sea.

"I met m'amie, Nicole, in Rimouski. We played with our dolls together, took them to school and often left them to camp out under the bridge at the creek. We each had a carriage to carry our dolls. That's what you use doll carriages for when you're ten."

I'm sad, and frightened, thought the boy. And this woman is talking on about dolls.

"I'm curious," said Milli, "about my Sophia. She's my favourite horse, and now my only horse. She has been behaving oddly. Do you think she might be ill? Do you know about horses?"

Milli's voice was soft, inviting, calming. The boy felt a stillness enter the room. The demons seemed to retreat a little.

"I don't know," the boy mumbled.

"She used to prance with excitement when I saddled her up, my Sophia. Now, when I ride her, she's poky. Her eyes droop. Her head is down. Do you suppose she may be sick? Do you suppose she may be hurt? Do you imagine that she could be sad? Her eyes look sad. Do you think horses get sad, like children?"

This woman talks funny, the boy thought.

"Where's my mom?" the boy asked.

"Your mother's with the doctor, and your sister. He is a good doctor and very smart. He is a specialist actually. Do you know what a specialist does?"

"They cut people open."

"Some do. I think Sophia might need an operation, or she might have to take some medicine that might taste bad. I suppose Sophia could die if a doctor can't make her better. Sometimes horses die because the doctor can't make them better. Your sister's doctor is a very fine doctor though. I'm sure he will make her better. I have worked with him for many years.

"I need to get Sophia to a doctor. Do you know what they call doctors that treat horses? They call them veterinarians. That's a big word. I need to get Sophia to a veterinarian. The veterinarian, he treats horses so they get better. The doctor will help your sister get better. Do you think Sophia might need an operation?"

"I don't know."

Milli sat down beside the boy. He welcomed the closeness.

"Do you know what I think? I think Sophia is fine, not sick. I think Sophia is sad though. She is alone now. Our other horse had to go. We couldn't keep her. She was too wild, too much work. She's at a ranch in the rolling grasslands of the Alberta foothills, a place with more room to run. Sophia doesn't know what happened to her friend. She doesn't understand where she's gone. I think Sophia is sad, and I think she's afraid too. When we don't understand we sometimes become sad and afraid. Horses, too.

"I miss my friend, Nicole, after all these years. Do you know how it feels to miss someone you love?"

"I miss my mom. Where's Nicole?" the boy asked.

"Nicole left me many years ago. They said that she must go to Montreal to a hospital there, for sick children. She didn't say goodbye. She never came back. I'm sure she would have if she could. For a while I imagined that she had ridden off on a beautiful white mare named Sophia, and that one day she would return on that same mighty mare. But she didn't.

"Her mother and father never came back either. I think they decided that if they couldn't come back with Nicole, they weren't coming back. Rimouski was no longer a place where they wanted to be. It was no longer a place where I wanted to be either, sans Nicole.

"I cried when Nicole left. Crying is a way to share your sadness with others. It is a way to release the ache we feel deep inside when we are sad and afraid, when we have a hurt heart. If we don't cry we continue to ache. Sometimes it is easier to cry than talk. Crying is an easier way to share our grief, sometimes.

"You have probably heard someone say that 'boys don't cry.' You don't believe it. I've seen boys cry, just like girls. They're better for it. It is a good way for boys to share their sadness. There need be no shame.

Milli continued. "Once I understood that Nicole was not coming back, after I cried, I knew what I would do. Some in town said I grew up. Of course I didn't become big just then. That took many more years. But I grew in the way I *thought*, I became more considerate of others, responsible, I made serious plans for my life. It was when I realized life wasn't just about me, and Nicole.

"Do you understand? It can be complicated for a young boy of ten. Are you ten years old?" asked Milli rhetorically.

"At that time I decided to put away my dolls and become a nurse. I thought if I became a nurse I could go to that hospital and find and care for my dear friend, Nicole."

"Did you find Nicole?"

"I became a nurse. I have found many Nicoles."

"Is my sister one of your Nicoles?" the boy asked of Nurse Milli.

"Other friends in Rimouski said Nicole was a valiant girl, like a great white mare. She was brave, and gave everyone in Montreal that knew her, happiness and joy. I was told that everyone who met Nicole loved her, and that their love was returned."

"Is my sister one of your Nicoles?" the boy asked again.

"Yes young man. Your sister is one of my Nicoles. She is a courageous young lady just like my friend."

"Is Nicole, I mean my sister, going to get better and come home? Or is she going to be as your friend and not come back?" asked the boy.

"Would you like your sister to come home? Do you believe your sister will come home?"

"Yeah, I do." The boy spoke with certainty.

"Then your sister will come home. Your sister will be fine. I'm sure of it. Now though, your sister needs your mother. And you need to be brave. You can cry if you want, but you can not be weak. You need to show courage. Nicole taught me that before she got sick."

Nurse Milli put her arm over the boy's shoulders, and pulled him close.

The demons had left the room.

Take a Deep Breath

By Jody Chadderton

I was still standing up taking my coat off when the train started, so of course it seemed to lurch forward and I almost fell right into the lap of the nice young man sitting across from me—well he looked nice, anyway—I hadn't yet met him had I because I hadn't even sat down yet, then the train rumbled along and I got used to the rhythm, then I actually did meet the man across from me and he was nice just as I thought he would be and it turned out he was going to Welwyn too and he had just been down in London visiting his parents and you know he looked just like our Joey, or at least what Joey looked like when he was a young man and maybe that's why I knew from the start he was nice and wasn't it just my luck to have such an attractive young stranger to chat with on the journey, so we talked about how things have changed in London over the last few years and about the latest theatre offerings and the gallery shows and the Henry Moore sculptures in Kensington Gardens and then we talked about tennis and horseracing and he's a cricket player himself and he's interested in all kinds of sports and he makes his living as a book critic for some magazine I've never heard of, but that surprised me because I read all sorts of magazines, so I found out all about him and he about me I suppose and before I knew it we were pulling into the Welwyn station and I hadn't even pulled my knitting out.

Too Many Miracles

By Sue Whittaker

When our Michael was born
in the spring of the year
our Miracle Baby
after so many tears . . .

We studied his toes
there were ten of the best,
blue eyes like yours,
you puffed out your chest.

Those blue eyes turned brown
but, no bother, by then
we were happily informed
to expect little Ben.

Well, Ben had the colic,
I ne'er saw my bed,
so how we had Declan,
"Sure, a miracle!" we said.

Three sets of wee toes
soon grew to be five.
Mary Margaret was twins!
Two girls in our lives.

Fifty wee digits!
My Pat worked two jobs.
Days, cutting peat,
nights, driving Nobs.

Siobhan was the next
to make us feel blessed.
Ten fingers, ten toes,
to add to the rest.

Sixty cute digits
to fit into shoes,
and knit pairs of sox for,
when Doc brought the news.

"Plan nothing for New Years,
you'll not make the dance!"
And wasn't he crack on!
I gave birth to Nance.

Seventy pinkies
tucked in at night.
The days were a blur
and the money was tight.

Then along came our Seamus
making it eighty.
(well, 81 actually, Seamus was full of surprises)
Then *Pat* saw the doctor
helping things greatly!

Now we kneel for God's blessing
and we take up two rows.
A twenty foot family
with one hundred . . . one . . . toes.

Views

By Anita L. Trapler

Runners run,
that's what they do.
Walkers walk,
to take in views.

Excitement on the Ranch

By Maureen Olson

"Hi Mom, we've just arrived. It took us eight hours which wasn't bad. The pass had been plowed. Is there anything I can do for you before you get home?"

"I'll be leaving the office in about a half hour. If your Dad hasn't lit the living room fire, would Henry do it, please?"

There was snow on the ground and a cold wind blowing down Okanagan Lake. A crackling fire would be much appreciated.

It took Henry three trips to the wood pile to carry in enough wood for the evening. A gust of cold air blew in every time he opened the door but in no time at all he had a roaring fire going. We were enjoying the warmth and were almost ready to take off our coats when Mom arrived home, rushed in the front door and shouted, "Leave the door open!"

Surprised, I did. Mom ran to the fireplace, grabbed the unlit end of a piece of burning wood in her bare hand, hustled across the room and through the open door, then chucked the flaming log out in the snow.

"Chimney fire," she yelled. "Get all those logs outside! We have to put the fire out!"

My husband, Henry, looked confused.

Mom snarled, "What were you thinking, building a fire that size?"

To my father, Jimmie, she barked, "Call the Fire Department!"

We were three miles from town with no fire hydrants and a volunteer Fire Department which had to be summoned. Frozen with fear, I waited with Mom and Dad, listening to the roaring of the fire in the chimney, unable to do anything.

Henry, a man of action, wrestled a ladder up against the house. He clambered onto the roof and climbed up to the chimney. There were no flames rising into the darkening sky, but a great heat rose from deep down. The creosote deposited in the chimney from past fires was aglow.

The fire engine and water-filled pumper truck were welcome sights when they finally arrived. From inside the house we could hear the stomping of feet on the roof as the firemen climbed up to the chimney to pump water down the opening. Henry told me to get towels and watch for water flowing down into the fireplace. I watched with apprehension thinking the living room would be flooded.

But only steam appeared. Once the tank was empty, the firemen left. The Chief told Mom to call again if things heated up. They were not sure the fire was out.

We settled down to a late, cold dinner. Conversation was stilted. Mom fumed. We cowered, and within two hours we heard the rumble in the chimney start up again. We called the Fire Department. This time they inserted a hose with a spray nozzle down the chimney. Again, no water appeared in the fireplace, just steam. Confident that they had completely extinguished the fire this time, the firemen left in an hour.

We slept fitfully, keeping an ear out for the ominous rumble of a chimney fire but the rest of the night was uneventful.

A day later, Henry and I left to make the long trip back home. Henry was very aware of Mom's lingering displeasure with him. Now he understood why we never built a roaring fire in the fireplace.

Three weeks later, Mom phoned and asked to speak to Henry.

"Thank you, Henry," she began, "for all your hard work on the night of the fire. The insurance company came through for us. They covered the cost of cleaning the entire downstairs, including the drapes and the rugs! I've never had such a clean house for so little effort."

Henry laughed, picturing her heroic effort to remove the burning logs from the fireplace.

"You earned every penny of it," he declared.

I Am the Roll of Fat

By Maureen Kresfelder

I am the roll of fat
ensconced above Maureen's belly.
I will not move because
I get more saturated fat
and attention
than all the other rolls
put together.
Besides, moving is stressful
and Maureen has enough stress
in her life right now.
I will support her,
remain faithful,
something she can count on,
something she can blame
on poor metabolism,
or heredity,
or misaligned stars.

But at my cellular level,
I know one day
Maureen will betray me:
she will shed me
like a winter coat when
she has found her spring.

The Music Man

By Anita L. Trapler

He died an old man. He did. I wept. He was not one who wanted anybody to shed tears over him. Nevertheless, tears fell from my eyes and splashed onto his dusty casket. All this, before I used the backhoe to lower the coffin into the ground.

I, Johnny Kinkaid, had just turned fifteen in 1960 when my uncle died. We always had our secrets. Uncle Vinson made me swear to never tell anyone where he was buried. Not my dad, who was the youngest and his only brother, nor his two sisters, must know about his body's final resting place.

My Uncle Vinson lay beneath a stately fir tree beside an electrified barbed wire fence which kept Dad's cattle back from the road. The grave was unmarked save for a few yellow ribbons tied to the branches of the tree.

I said my last "goodbyes" and "may God be with you" and returned the backhoe just as I had found it in my dad's machine shed.

Uncle Vinson always had been a prankster. His death and memorial service was his kind of joke played out upon his family. Catherine, Vinson's younger sister, had complained, "I've never attended a funeral with no casket nor a body to view." From out of her black handbag, she withdrew a white handkerchief, blew her nose and dabbed at her eyes. "Humph!" she said. "In my view this memorial service, or whatever it is, is not a real funeral." The solemn ushers, all wearing black suits moved to calm her down.

I dearly loved this man who grew up through the Great Depression. He earned his coin by playing on street corners, in dance halls, and at church box socials. Although my uncle had never taken a music lesson on any instrument, he taught himself to strum guitars, pick on banjos, chord on organs and pianos and play the fiddle. He also banged on drums and cymbals and sang along with the best of them.

The odd time, just for the fun of it, he'd enter a fiddling contest. More often than not, he walked away with first or second prize: a free meal ticket for two, or tickets for two to a movie house.

My Uncle Vinson was a tall, broad-shouldered man whose too few black and grey pinstriped suits were worn and shiny. He rarely changed his oxblood lace-up shoes for any other pair, or colour or style. His favourite hat was a grey fedora with a black hat band decorated with a couple of rooster feathers.

Ever since I'd known my Uncle Vinson, he never had his hair cut. He wore it styled into a single braid, which ran down his back to his waist.

I can hear him clearly now. He'd say, "Johnny, Johnny, come here. Sit down on the piano bench beside me and we'll make some music. Together." At that time I was about five years old and I loved to be with my Uncle Vinson. Within ten to fifteen minutes I could chord along or do upper scale notes to songs like *Pop Goes the Weasel, Yankee Doodle, Onward Christian Soldiers* and *Oh Dem Golden Slippers.*

Making music with my uncle was so much fun. We laughed, clapped and tapped out rhythms. For a little extra fun we jazzed up some nursery rhymes too.

When I was around ten or eleven years old, Uncle Vinson and I could rap out almost any musical style.

Rock 'n' roll was just taking off. My uncle loved Chuck Berry, Bill Haley and the Comets, Elvis Presley and Buddy Holly. He roared along with, *You Ain't Nothin' but a Hound Dog. Peggy Sue* was a favourite too. My uncle was so cool. However, his love for the song *The Great Pretender* was intense. I sensed in him a longing and a loneliness buried deep in his heart. I too, was a great pretender, and I sure never asked my uncle about anything personal.

Then trouble started. My mom, she'd speak loudly behind carelessly closed doors, her voice sometimes pitched to high "C." One day I stopped to listen. I could see Mom and Dad from where I stood in the hall.

"Johnny will turn out an ambitionless bum and no account. Just like his Uncle Vinson. Derek, do you want him to become a worthless troubadour? Eating in dingy cafes, crashing strangers' houses? Or worse, playing for peanuts on the streets?"

Mom reached for a fresh packet of cigarettes. "Johnny's spending too much time with that no-good brother of yours. He's too busy plucking a guitar or banging on drums to tend to his homework."

My dad's dark eyes sparked. I knew I shouldn't be eavesdropping or spying on them but all their conversations lately were centered on me. "Madeleine, get off the pot. Johnny's got real talent. When we scrape the dough together, we're going to see that the boy takes music lessons. Guitar or whatever instrument he fancies. Then, he'll outperform my brother."

Mom began chewing her thumbnail. When my mother became angry or upset, she always bit her fingernails.

I stifled a sneeze and continued to observe my parents through the partly opened bedroom door.

I thought, why can't my mother have any vision at all? Does every dream in this house have to belong to her alone?

I knew my mother completely disapproved of me because I wanted to be a musician, just like my uncle. But there was some other reason too, why she resented me. She sure couldn't love me uncondition- ally like my friend Joey's mom did him. I didn't think Mom would ever approve of me unless I turned into a well-educated businessman.

Now, more than ever, whenever my parents quarreled, I was the center of all their fights.

But my Uncle Vinson had been, in one word, a "nonjudgmental" man and I'd adored him. My dad came a close second. But there was something not right. I knew it. There was a secret about me so carefully concealed and covered over, just like there was of my Uncle Vinson's gravesite.

One day I walked down the hall, tossed my backpack onto the kitchen counter and reached for a glass of milk. I felt thirsty and tired from a long day at school. Miss Willows, my Grade Five teacher, had been so cross and miserable. She had threatened everyone with detentions after school.

My mother entered the room prepared to clean the kitchen windows. She stopped and stood with her hands on her hips and glared at me.

"You're late, again. Where were you? With your dearly beloved Uncle Vinson?"

"Yeah, Mom. We're practicing for a school dance."

"What?"

I shrugged. "That's what I said, Mom." I tried not to sound sassy.

"Johnny, you're a kid, only ten years old. What's going on?"

"The dance is for high-school kids, Mom. It's a school dance. A fundraiser for the school. Many of the other kids' parents will be there."

I looked up. Hopefully.

Mom wiped her hands on her apron. Her face was flushed and her hands were reddened by some cleaning solution she'd been using.

"Well, you won't be seeing your dad and me at that dance. Will you, Johnny?"

Again, I shrugged my shoulders, downed the glass of milk, grabbed my backpack and hastily ran up the stairs to my room. If Mom died tomorrow, I'd not shed any tears over her grave. Besides, she drank too much, and the liquor made her nasty and bitter. She seemed a little nicer to my dad. But not much. He just couldn't see or cared not to see her nasty side.

Years later, in late October, my dad telephoned the university Conservatory of Music. He said he'd meet me at the front entrance. The tone of his voice scared me.

Dad's battered red Chevy pickup skidded to a sudden stop. "Hurry, Johnny. Get in. We haven't much time, or so the doctors believe. Your mother is in the Intensive Care Unit at the hospital. She has had a heart attack and she insists on seeing you now."

"Will Mom be all right? Will she die? Shit. I . . . don't want her to die."

Dad's black eyes teared. He parked near the entrance to the hospital and we approached the Admissions desk.

"Mr. Kinkaid, your wife is in room 212, but we don't . . ."

Dad grabbed my arm and we raced up the stairs. Mom was awake and attached to many tubes as well as a heart monitor. Her thin, pale arms reached out for me.

I wanted to shrink back. I wanted to run away from her.

"Derek," she sighed, "could I be alone with Johnny? Just for a few minutes?"

Dad sadly turned away and walked out of the room.

"Mom – I . . ."

"Sh–sh–sh, Johnny. There's so much you need to know about."

"I think it's about time!"

"Johnny, you're my son. Your Uncle Vinson … is …"

I tried to be gentle. "Mom, he's dead. He is my late uncle. What are you going to criticize him for now?"

"Johnny, Vinson was not your uncle."

"Mom, I always knew you despised him. But not this much."

My mother's eyes were a pale green with yellowish flecks. Her eyes were her most beautiful feature. Now, her eyes were red rimmed, with deep purple puffy marks beneath them.

"Johnny, Vinson . . . was your real father."

I exclaimed, "Derek is my dad. What are you talking about? Uncle Vinson was Dad's brother."

50

"Johnny, until now, I've never told anyone the truth. Yes, Derek raised you. He has always suspected that you were really Vinson's son, but he wanted to protect you, above all."

I choked back sobs. I didn't want to cry and especially not in front of my mother.

Mom's voice dropped to barely a whisper. I wanted her to stop what she was saying to me. I jerked away from her.

"Johnny," she pleaded, "hear me out before it's too late." Tears streamed down her cheeks.

"During the war, Derek and I married two years before he was sent from Brandon to Germany. He was gone eighteen months cleaning up Hitler's debris. His Company tramped throughout Holland and France. At the beginning of August 1944, he was sent home on a three-week leave. Then he was gone again." Mom deeply sighed and closed her eyes. She became so still, I was frightened. Just as I was ready to ring for the nurse, Mom's eyes opened wide.

"I loved Derek so much, but in no time at all he was listed MIA. When a black vehicle drove up to our apartment building, I knew there would be no good news. And there wasn't."

"What happened, Mom?" I was really scared now.

"You're Uncle Vinson came calling. He told me he loved me, too. And that he wanted to marry me. We became very close.

"But I couldn't let go of Derek. My memories of him were too strong. Then I found I was pregnant with you, Johnny, and so you were born in the month of May, 1945.

"Months later I was notified that Derek was alive. He was on his way home.

"He was so happy he had an infant son. But I believe, from the beginning, he guessed you were Vinson's child. It's just that you are so like Vinson in so many ways. But he never stopped loving you as his own."

My mother looked like a vulnerable child. I now understood. She never stopped hurting either.

She said, "I didn't hate Vinson. I was afraid the truth would come out and that Vinson would claim you. I love you, Johnny, with all of my heart. But you seemed to prefer your uncle's company over Derek's or mine. You appeared to love Vinson above all."

"Mom, what am I to do now?" I was wracked by sobs.

She smiled weakly and said, "Become the best musician you can be. That's what both your fathers would want."

Martha and the Gambler

By Sue Whittaker

Not far off, but getting more distant each moment, Martha could hear the drunken threats of Brummet Lorken, her stepfather, bouncing off the hills of Jackpot Valley. Wishing she could stay to see to the last resting place of her mother, newly dead that morning, she instead made the decision to attend to her own safety as her dying mother had advised. Leaving the burial in God's hands, she made her escape.

She could reasonably expect two days' head start. Brummet would drink until his supply of liquor ran out, then sleep for twelve hours or more and waste another day hung over and covering the same ground repeatedly, unable to believe she wouldn't appear to cook him a meal when he bellowed for service.

Thank God Aunt Eleanore had stepped in and taken her little brother, Jamie, away with her when she realized the end was near for her sister. His love of adventure would have been quickly overwhelmed by the rough terrain and thick underbrush she was forced to break through in the first hours of her getaway.

Following the creek to the bridge, she stumbled wet and cold, bruised and scratched on to the narrow dirt road leaving the valley. She trudged until daylight, waiting for the first wagons to appear, wending their way to Brownsville. There she would board the train, using the small sack of coins her mother had saved for Martha to buy a ticket to freedom.

She was able to dart out of the roadside bushes and boost herself on to the tailgate of a slow-moving mule-drawn farm wagon just as the sun came over the mountains. The wagoner didn't bother to acknowledge her presence and she kept her mouth shut. The ride to Brownsville was dusty and bone-rattling. She was parched by the time they arrived, but she was able to catch the morning train when it stopped to take on water, and she curled up and slept as they headed west and didn't move until she was forced to disembark or pay for the next leg of the journey. She chose to leave the train, and set out to explore the small town that warranted no name other than Whistle Stop.

Her filthy clothes, straggly hair and beaten look made her easy to ignore which was fine by her, except that as her limited resources ran out, she needed a job, which would require a level of acceptance. Whistle Stop was unable to provide either. She moved on from town, to farm, to ranch, always heading west. A few hours of work here and there, mucking out stables, carrying water, brushing and feeding horses, weeding and picking vegetables, had afforded her one small meal a day for a few weeks, but poor nutrition and little attention to hygiene were gaining a foothold. She had overcome her fear of being found and dragged back home, but a new desperation dogged her. Exhaustion, hunger and filth were taking their toll.

The last two of these scourges were alleviated the day she met Gertie Miller on the outskirts of a small river town called Royce's Landing.

"Yes, I have work for you," the owner of "Gertie's Room and Board" declared. "But first you get yourself a bath and wash those clothes."

What was meant to be a dictum sounded more like a blessing to Martha. "Yes, 'm," she croaked.

"What's your name, girl? I'm Gertie Miller."

"Martha, ma'am. I thank you for the chance to clean up."

"There's a dipper by the pump if you need a drink, Martha. I'll bring out the washtub and some hot water. You can cool it down from the pump. Then when you're clean, use the water to wash your clothes. There's a washboard," she said, pointing to the metal and wood apparatus propped up against the steps. "Pray those rags you're wearing survive the scrubbing." The worried look told Martha that while Gertie could afford a tub of bathwater, she was not likely to be able to replace a set of clothes.

After arranging Martha's open-air bath, Gertie said, "You can cover yourself with this robe while your clothes dry." She hung a cotton floral wrapper on a post within reach of the washtub, threw a rag mat down on the tufts of dried grass alongside the tub and dropped an old length of toweling and a scrap of soap on it. "Knock on the door when you're finished. I'll have something ready for you to eat. Then I'll check your hair for lice," she added.

With that, Gertie left Martha and went inside to her kitchen. Checking periodically through the back window to see how the bath was going, she was heartsick to see the rack of bones the young woman had become. She threw an extra pork chop in the frying pan. Well worth the company, she thought remembering her daughter, Anna, and the lost comfort of another person in the house.

After dinner, Gertie had Martha straddle a kitchen chair. Gertie lit a kerosene lantern and placed it where it would illuminate her field of study to the best advantage. Martha squirmed with the thought of what Gertie might find as she divided her long hair into tiny sections, looking for evidence of lice and their nits.

Eventually, the stark silence of the kitchen was broken by Gertie. "No bugs!" she stated. "Even they hate hair that dirty."

She showed Martha to a tiny little closet of a room off the kitchen. There was no window, but the bedding was clean and smelled of sunshine, and every surface in the room was scrubbed and shining. Martha was asleep before Gertie left the kitchen on her way through to her bedroom.

Martha attacked her housecleaning chores with real purpose the following week, an effort Gertie had to admire. Unfortunately, there were few customers to enjoy the sparkling windows, the gleaming furniture and the freshly laundered linens. They even took the stovepipe down from the kitchen range and banged the soot out of it in the back yard. Gertie feared fire more than anything. She told a few stories of families who had lost their homes from chimney fires, as the two of them bashed away, removing creosote from the lengths of stovepipe.

Martha was acutely aware of the lack of custom Gertie was attracting at this slow time of year, and the drain on resources that she represented. She needed another job. Gertie had suggested she might find work at the local saloon, as Gertie herself had, when she first came to town. Martha decided it was worth a shot, although a drinking establishment would have been her last choice considering her experience with her step-father.

Martha walked the short distance in to Royce's Landing on a lovely fall day. She made inquiries at Hoyle's Dry Goods, Hoyle's General Store and the Rialto Hotel but avoided the millinery, her apparel not being quite up to the mark.

Her eye was, however, drawn to a pair of moss green gloves that accompanied a fetching hat swathed in crisp netting, displayed in the window. The gloves looked to be a perfect match for Gertie's Sunday dress. How she would dearly love to be able to purchase those for her new friend and saviour.

She was easily recognized as "the girl helping out Gertie" by most people in the small town on the bank of the North Fork River. But times were hard, she could see that. And she had little to offer other than a willingness to do a good day's work for her pay. With her options dwindling, Martha took a position across the street from Cupid's Saloon to survey the action in the vicinity of the swinging doors. Other than the dawdling retreat of one scruffy farmer, picking his teeth and pulling his hat down to shade his eyes from the afternoon sun as he left the dark interior of the saloon, Martha saw nothing. She heard nothing.

Feeling somewhat calmed by the tranquility of the situation across the street, she wandered over with few hopes for employment but a growing curiosity regarding the inner workings of a drinking establishment. Adjusting her eyes to the gloomy interior, she saw two men slumped in wooden chairs at a small round table, several playing cards clasped before their chests. The only other motion in the room came from a haze of blue smoke and dust particles that floated across the stream of light coming in through a narrow window. Two mugs of beer on the table were the only signs of possible inebriation she could detect. The scene held no more threat of danger than had the inside of the General Store, the Dry Goods or the Hotel.

With only slight trepidation, she pushed through the swinging doors attracting the attention of the well-dressed gentleman facing her. He was in the process of spreading his playing cards on the table with one hand, scooping some coins toward him with the other. His opponent gulped the last of his beer, cursed his poor luck with good humour and picked up his hat to leave. He looked Martha over with little interest as he tipped his hat out of habit, and left, whistling his way down the street.

"Ma'am? You lost?" The question was laced with a hint of a smile and the huskiness of years of tobacco usage smoothed over by whiskey. Martha assumed he was the owner. He wore a black suit and white shirt. His string tie was loose and the top button on his shirt was undone. He looked to be tall; his legs extended quite some distance to the side of the table. He was lean with a wide expanse of shoulders, his face was tanned and his dark hair was streaked from the sun. His posture was relaxed, projecting an image of non-threatening indulgence or supreme laziness, Martha was unsure which. Now a half smile softened his narrow, intelligent-looking face and leant Martha some sense of ease. Brown eyes surveyed her with good-natured interest and more than a hint of devilry.

Gathering her wandering imagination, Martha replied, "No sir. Looking for work." She cut across the floor towards him.

"Yeah, I figured I saw you making your way down the street earlier. Can't help but notice that my establishment seems to have been your last choice."

How desperate did she appear to be, Martha wondered? Hopelessness was not a good bargaining chip, she sensed. Looking down at her clean but drab skirt, over-shirt and scuffed boots, there was nothing to suggest she was anything but poor with nowhere to turn. However, she did have one ace up her sleeve, she thought. Sometimes it was "who you knew."

"Gertie asks to be remembered to you," she burst out, smiling hopefully.

There was a long pause, then he asked, "Does she now? And how is Gertie these days?"

"She's real good. I bin working fer her this past week. Cleanin,' doin' laundry plus yard work and such." Martha gulped. Slipping into bad grammar was not going to help her situation. "I-I mean she is just fine. She is willing to put a good word in for me if anyone has need of my services," she stated, breathily. She watched a slow grin spread across the face of the gentleman before her.

"So Gertie sent you down here to offer your services, did she?" There was a definite twinkle in his eye now, Martha was quick to notice.

Why am I starting to feel like a rabbit in a snare, she wondered? Her good sense was telling her to bow out of this conversation, which seemed just a little beyond her full comprehension and made her feel a bit squirmy, to be honest. But on the other hand, as the proprietor rose from his chair, straightening his vest and running his fingers through his hair, how often did she get to feast her eyes on such a sterling example of manliness? Said "sterling example" was now standing before her, resting his weight on one hip and obviously waiting for her to speak. One eyebrow rose. He pinned her in place with a look.

"Oh," said Martha, "Gertie! Yes! Gertie said that sometimes you had need of help. But you don't look too busy here, so I guess unless there is work to be done above, you don't need me, sir. So I'll keep looking . . ." And she turned to go.

"Just a minute. You haven't even introduced yourself."

"I'm Martha. Martha Burns. And you are?" she inquired, as she stopped and turned.

"Royce," he said. "Call me Royce."

"Oh, sir, I couldn't do that! Mr. . . ." she suggested, raising her hands toward him.

"Mr. Loramer is my old man," he said briskly. "I go by Royce here in town."

"Hm," said Martha, the light coming on. "Royce's Landing! Were you named after it or was the town named after you?"

There was another long silence. Finally, "That's been a hard one for me to live down," he said.

Martha looked around her at the bare, sticky floorboards, the dirty windows then she sniffed. "It looks like a person could live a lot down in this place," she commented.

After a rather stunned look, he threw his head back and laughed. "From the mouths of the unemployed," he gasped, pushing hair back from his eyes. "That was blunt. Does this approach get you many jobs?"

"I've learned to say what I think, working for Gertie."

Yes, Royce thought, I can see Gertie's hand in this. She came in here and took over when I was well on my way to losing everything. She was a mother and father to me well after the time I should have needed parents. She whipped the saloon into shape and me along with it. The drinking was under control now and it was time for a new challenge. Is this what Gertie had sent him? A new challenge? There was probably no harm in exploring the possibilities. For the size of her, Miss Martha seemed to have a lot of iron in her spine.

"So which was it?"

"I . . . pardon?" he asked, struggling back to the present.

"So which came first, you or Royce's Landing?" Martha asked, rolling her eyes.

"'Bout the same time," he admitted. "My mother went into labour on the trip up the river. They just got her on dry land and I was born."

"Ah!" she said, "Royce's Landing. Someone had a sense of humour at the time. Having attended a couple of births, I'm betting it wasn't your mother."

"Not then and never after," said Royce. "She hated this place from the day she was first exposed to it, you might say. It took her twenty-three years and many long visits away for her to convince my father to join her back east. It was only after I returned from my schooling, that my father gave in and left the town to me."

"You own the town?"

"Lock, stock and barrel," he said. "My father bought the land, laid out the streets, and built the Dry Goods, the General Store, the Hotel and this saloon. The Gold Rush was headed this way at the time. Unfortunately it took a detour."

"Boy, that must have cost a lot of money, to build a town."

"Fortunately, my mother's family, the Hoyles, has plenty of it."

"So you've been left in charge? It appears you have a habit of quitting early," she said, looking around disdainfully.

Something changed in his face. She thought she might have over-stepped her mark.

"Martha, you look like a person who might be willing to take a risk," he said. "How about we have a little game of Five Card Stud? You win, you get to be in charge here. I win, you work for me."

"You're offering me a job then?" Martha thought she should be very clear about his intentions. He had the look of the cat that swallowed the canary about him.

"That I am," he replied, placing his hand at the back of her waist and ushering her over to a relatively clean table that held a deck of cards. "What do you know about cards?" he asked.

"I play gin rummy," she said.

"Good enough," he allowed. "We each get five cards. The player with the highest score, wins."

"That's it?" she asked. "That won't take much time."

"Count on it," he replied. "You don't look like you have much to bet with anyway."

"Just these three smooth stones that my little brother gave me before we parted," she said, fishing them out of her shirt pocket.

"Guess that's my stake!" She laughed and set them on the table between them.

Royce paused before dealing. If he were going to have any qualms about this transaction, this would be the time to call it off.

Nah! She looked old enough to know what she was doing. Eighteen, maybe nineteen. And besides that she had been practically daring him to make a move. So this was it. She would be in his pocket in less time than it took to name him and the town.

It was a close thing. She was luckier than she looked. Without the second king that he drew, he'd have had nothing. Her long straight fell short of a middle four, dashing her hopes and leaving her biting on her lower lip.

"You can have these," he said, pushing the three pebbles towards her. He got up from the table and came around to pull out her chair. You couldn't say he wasn't a gentleman. He gently steered her towards the stairs that led to the second floor. With each step up that they took, she became a bit more rigid and harder to propel forward.

"Maybe you could tell me what you have in mind for me to do," she said, digging her heels in as they reached the top of the stairs.

He reached around her to open a bedroom door from the landing. She froze.

"If that's to be my room, I'm not sleeping there until those bedcovers are washed!" She balked, and without picking her up, he doubted he'd get her past the door.

"Well, Martha, we aren't here to sleep. I have other things in mind for you, darlin.'" He swept her long braid aside and ran a string of kisses along the back of her neck. She twisted in his arms and faced him, practically spitting with rage.

"What is the matter with you! Just tell me what you have in mind for me, and I'll get on with it. A 'please' is plenty. Let me go!"

Could she possibly be this naïve, he wondered? What did she think went on above a saloon? She looked a little scared. Maybe she needed some time to warm up to him.

"It's alright," he tried to assure her. "I'll lie down and you can sit by me and we'll talk."

"Boy, it's no wonder this place is a mess," she said. "Lying on the bed in the middle of the day! Talking? You are never going to get a day's work out of anyone if this is the kind of boss you are."

He pulled her down on top of him and tried to shut her up by kissing her. She went as rigid as a pistol and when he opened his eyes she was staring at him like he was the worst kind of vermin she had ever encountered.

"This is never going to work," he said, admitting defeat. As vermin went, his line looked to be slated for extinction.

"Can you cook?" he asked. "Perhaps your place is in the kitchen."

"Food!" she declared, ignoring the reference to her "place" in life. "My specialty." She kissed him on the nose, leapt off the bed, rushed out the door and flew down the stairs, calling, "Does this place have a kitchen?"

He wasn't absolutely sure but he thought he'd been outplayed. Good thing there was a wood range and a sink with a pump in the room behind the bar. Maybe he'd have more luck demanding dinner in the kitchen than the pleasure of her company in the bedroom. And tomorrow was another day. Watch out Martha! He might quit early but he always showed up for work. And she was his next project.

<u>Granny Drivers</u>

By Jody Chadderton

When I think of Granny drivers
I think of Grandma's blue Buick
power everything
long before dreams
of power anything:
windows, locks, seats,
plus tilt, cruise
and a gizmo on the speedometer
that lets you know if you speed.
Let's say the speed limit is 60
(before they invented km/h)
you set it for 65,
when you reach 65 it screeches,
really Loud Horrible Noise
so you set it at 70.
After all, you have to speed to pass.

One thing Grandma didn't have
was air conditioning,
unnecessary extravagance in New Westminster, no doubt.
But Fraser Canyon in mid-July
counting tunnels: Alexandra, Saddle Rock, China Bar,
seven in all.

Windows open for the breeze,
blue chiffon scarf
draped over left shoulder
for sunshade.
Whoosh! Gone.
Gram does a brief shoulder check,
says, "Oh, dear,"
and powers on . . . .

A Full Life

By Allene Halliday

My Life has indeed been a bed of roses.
But these blooms aren't like those
found shorn of sharp edges in a florist's.
No, the bounty from my life's garden
has an abundance of prickly thorns
to complement the charming blossoms.

Nana's Beans
An Epiphany for Young Bobby

By Everett J. Marwood

Her home was tiny as compared to our big old farmhouse, and grey like many others on the street. Come to think of it, her home was, in many ways, like all others in the neighbourhood. Looking ahead, down the tree-lined boulevard, you could see one home, then another, all indistinguishable from each other. I had been told that they had been built decades earlier, in the forties, designed plain and built with economy during difficult years. They were constructed to house the factory workers building the machinery of war.

"We are here boys. Get your things together," Mother said, and then added, "I want you to behave like angels or there will be trouble. Nana won't tolerate any rowdiness."

The roof had a steep slope with tiny gabled windows that peered out. The lower story of her home was barely visible from the street, hidden behind the tangled overgrown shrubs and ivy that cluttered the entranceway to the home.

Even a young child like myself could recognize that the home was in an unfortunate state of disrepair, with sagging troughs and curled shingles. The window frames, the few that you could see from the roadway, were bordered with peeling paint. The crumbling concrete walkway led to disintegrating steps and a weathered doorway.

"I'm telling you boys. I want you to be very quiet. You are here to be seen, not heard," Mother warned. "Nana's old and she likes it quiet." This was Mother's final admonishment before we entered Nana's home.

As on other visits, we let ourselves in when Nana called out from the kitchen, "Come in. The door is open." She was always in the crowded kitchen when my brothers, Mom and I arrived to visit. Inside, we huddled together in the small foyer until our shoes were removed and placed in an orderly row.

Every time I entered her home, and this time was no different, I was overwhelmed with the fragrances of my favourite foods, roast chicken or beef, and a freshly baked apple or pumpkin pie. Nana catered to our appetites.

In Nana's living room, the big crystal vase was again on the corner table, displaying a selection of freshly cut flowers from her garden. Serving spoons hung randomly from hooks above an old wooden cabinet.

A Bible was prominently displayed on a center table but its condition suggested it was seldom read. Corner tables were cluttered with novels and magazines. So were the chairs. Mom scurried about to clear places for us, then instructed us on where each of us was to sit. I sat down and quietly recovered an old issue of *Readers' Digest* from the table beside me, then pretended to browse the magazine.

Us boys behaved differently here than we did at home where obedience was more optional, rules less strict, and roughhousing occasionally allowed. This behavior would never be acceptable at Nana's home.

In time Nana came out of the kitchen and sat in the chair mother had earlier cleared for her. I looked up from my magazine. Nana looked at me and graciously said, "Good afternoon, Bobby." With my head lowered and my eyes raised, I timidly looked up at her and smiled in response.

If you studied her features you would have described her as stern. Emotions were rarely visible on her face. I fixed my stare. Nana's arms, elbows, and knees, were rough and gnarled like the old trees I shinnied up at home. Her nose was of average size I noted, but it bore the profile of the washboard she kept in the corner of her kitchen.

Her hair was grey, nearing white, but neatly groomed. She was sitting next to the window and today the sun's rays gave it a colouring I could not adequately describe. Her face was wrinkled of course, as she was old. And her clothes were not stylish like my mother's. I noticed these things yet none seemed to matter to me.

"Bobby is doing well in school," my mother said. "He likes his geography lessons in particular. His teacher is a young man just out of college." They spoke of me as though I was not present, which annoyed me a little, but in a short time I became distracted from the conversation.

An insect buzzed about, a fly, I presumed. Watching it awhile, I determined that if I were quick I could swat it and knock it to the floor. I knew I shouldn't. I knew that mother wouldn't approve. I knew the temptation was strong. I knew that I would succumb, in spite of the consequences I feared. I reshuffled my posture, preparing to lunge.

I surprised myself at how fast I could strike and in an instant the fly was stunned, and on the floor. Mother scolded for the distraction, silently this time, with her eyes, only, as this was my first offence. The fly recovered quickly and flew away. I regained my proper composure thankful that I had escaped a more severe chastening.

Nana glanced at me, and grinned. She quietly went to the kitchen and returned with the old fly swatter I had seen her use on many occasions. She handed it to me. "I don't like those pesky flies around," Nana said to me. I interpreted that comment to be the permission I sought.

Holding it for a few minutes, unsure of my next move, I feigned interest in the conversation of the moment. "Bobby is so well behaved," Mother continued. "He is never any trouble in school or at home."

It's on the window! I could see it! That pesky fly is on the window! In seconds the enemy would be crushed, vanquished by the invincible Superbility Bob. He grabbed his mystery weapon and leapt at the creature, and with one decisive strike Superbility Bob had destroyed the mighty beast and eliminated the threat to all mankind.

I expected applause. I received a rebuke.

"Bobby, sit down and be quiet!" Mother admonished. "You are going to annoy Nana." I feared the scolding would continue but it was interrupted when Nana announced; "I have something for you boys."

She again left for the kitchen and returned with four drinking straws, and a handful of small white pea beans. As my brothers and I obediently opened our palms she gave each of us some beans, and a straw. She placed a bean in the straw she had kept for herself, and with one strong blow she fired that bean into my right shoulder. Then she laughed the loudest laugh. "Let's have some fun boys. I'm on Bobby's team," shouted Nana.

"Nana, don't encourage them," Mother protested. "They'll be causing a big commotion in no time."

"Too late," Nana responded. She took another breath and beaned my brother in the center of his back as he turned to defend himself. The rumpus had begun. And during that very special afternoon, for the first time I could remember, my grandmother charmed and delighted me in a frivolous manner. I had never before imagined her to be a person fond of revelry.

The End of an Era

By Maureen Olson

An excavator rumbled off the trailer and on to the ground. Under my husband's directions it moved slowly to the first row of the Gala block of apple trees. The operator raised the boom to push against the trunk of the first tree. Over it went to be picked up, shaken to remove the clinging soil, then cast aside. The systematic removal of the trees had begun. I couldn't keep watching.

We had discussed the pros and cons of removing these trees for many months. We had been watching the cash return from Galas diminish over the last five years. They had produced a good crop yearly, but the payments from the packing house were disappointing. Over the same period, our costs had increased. The economic arguments were strong. But . . . .

As I walked back to the house I remembered the excitement we felt seven years ago when we brought the grafted cuttings for the new apple block. The holes had been prepared using an auger on the tractor, but we needed to loosen the base of each hole by hand to promote growth. One of us held the tree to center the roots in the hole, the other one shoveled soil around the root ball to stabilize it while we watered it in. It was satisfying to look the length of a completed row. We continued all day until all the trees were planted.

Each spring we savoured the glory of the pink and white blossoms. We thinned the fruit during the summer months to develop the best for the market.

In the fall we enjoyed picking those Galas, pleased with the quality of the fruit the trees produced and silently hoping for good markets.

In the end, all I could feel was sadness and disappointment. The trees were piled up like a funeral pyre. As the smoke from the fire ascended into the fall sky, so did my dreams.

I took a deep breath.

We plan to plant an excellent variety of grapes in the spring. So begins a new cycle.

Second Time Around

By Sue Whittaker

My sister Lynn and I might have been a bit over-confident when we insisted that Mom accompany Dad to Australia to attend the World Council of Forensic Scientists. Since Dad was delivering a paper, he deserved a cheering section. It might have worked out fine if the trip had been in the fall or winter of my sister's last year in high school. Unfortunately, things were heating up by the time I, her big brother, "took charge" in May.

Mom and Lynn had spent way too many days shopping for a ball gown, a dress appropriate for an afternoon tea, and all the shoes and other doo-dads so important to the first major coming-of-age celebration that my sister was careening toward. Lynn had sworn that everything would be fine, that Mom could not possibly pass up an opportunity to visit Auz and the family she had left behind before we were born. I promised Mom I would be with Lynn at every event in our parent's place. But things were starting to unravel.

First, Lynn's boyfriend, Derek, dumped her, leaving her scrambling for an escort to the Graduation Ball. To give Lynn credit, she dealt with it quite well. Yes, she took some liberties with his name and had written a very pointed "Opinion" piece in the school paper that might or might not have pertained to Derek the Dipstick, but on the whole she was staying focused.

Then, of course, she thought that every locker-side conversation that petered out as she approached, had to do with the big breakup. And most of the kids had made their plans for the Ball, so she had very few options as far as a new date went.

However, her old friend Ernie stepped up to the plate, when the girl he might have asked, got appendicitis.

Ernie was a nice enough guy but I couldn't see him fulfilling all Lynn's expectations on the big night. He couldn't dance, he could barely walk and talk at the same time and he couldn't keep a shirt tucked in, ever. It's not that he had no social skills, they were just at a very informal level. They did not include fancy footwork, small talk or fashion sense. There was a reason why Lynn and Dapper Derek were an item for a while. It was hard for me to see Ernie stepping into those shoes, however briefly.

Lynn has always shown a lot of empathy for Ernie. They became playmates when they were both toddlers, and she had made accommodations for his chronic asthma for a long time. During their pre-teen years, when the inflammation in his lungs was really bad, she would sit quietly with him playing board games or catching him up on homework. They read books in a tree house, rather than race around the neighbourhood when he wasn't up to it. They went swimming rather than biking when he was wheezy.

She was still keeping an eye out for him. Lynn was the first one at his side when he collapsed at a Junior High track meet during a 5K run. She had him on his feet, hunched over, taking deep drags on his inhaler before anyone else knew what was happening. That she had given up the female lead in the run meant little to her in light of her friend's struggle to breathe. They withdrew from the field together and found a place in the shade where Ernie could recover. I watched the whole episode from my station at the high jump pit and wished, a bit wistfully, that I had a friend so attuned to my needs.

But when Lynn wanted romance she looked elsewhere. You could see that Ernie didn't though. His eyes never left her when she was anywhere near him, poor guy.

With this big evening coming up, I could see the potential for a busted heart. Young women, in my experience, see themselves on the arm of their own version of Prince Charming on big occasions. It seemed inevitable that Ernie would fall short of the mark. Knowing that the opinion of her older brother would hold little sway with Lynn, I kept my peace.

Well, we made it through "The Tea," although I felt like a skunk at a garden party largely because of my mechanic's hands. I scrubbed until my cuticles bled but was unable to remove the entire build-up of grease. I had to give up a half-day's pay to be with Lynn but she thought we were really cool. Lynn's like that. So she was the only one there drinking tea with a guy! Who cared? Not her. The zanier the better, with Lynn.

Dad says it will land her in trouble one day, but I kind of admire her nerve and her happy-go-lucky attitude. She laughs more in a day than most people do in a month. She makes me laugh, even when I try to do the big brother thing and keep her in line.

Take this morning: I had to call her three times to get out of bed. She joins me for breakfast with her hair looking wild and weird. She's wearing, as far as I can tell, only a long Goofy t-shirt and she smiles at me with a front tooth blacked out. I nearly choked on my cereal.

"Jeez, Lynn," I said. "This is not Sadie Hawkins Day. What are you doing?"

"Well," she said. "I just got dumped, an old friend is probably not sleeping at nights dreading the fact that he has to pinch hit for Derek the Dork, so I am *not* going to school looking pitiful! Absurd, yes. But tragic, no. And keep your shirt on, Lyle. It's Pajama Day today."

I wouldn't let her out of the house until she put on a pair of jeans. Oh man! I thought. Mom really did deserve this vacation.

On the night of the Graduation Ball, Lynn transformed herself into an absolute babe without requiring any help from me except to secure the clasp of her necklace, thank God! She piled her mop of black curls up on the top of her head, adding years of sophistication to her usual look of "teenage casual." She wasn't generally into wearing much make-up but what she used

74

for the big occasion really made her dark eyes sparkle. Her milky skin appeared flawless.

Her gown must have been chosen while Mom snoozed from shopping exhaustion. No straps, no sleeves, no visible means of support!

Had Dad seen it? It was hard to believe it would have passed scrutiny with the founder of The League of Over-Protective Fathers.

I had to hope nobody sighed heavily around her or she'd be in danger of indecent exposure. Not to mention hypothermia, if the temperature dropped. No chance that would happen in a ballroom full of hormone-replete teens, I supposed. Arrrrgh! Next thing I knew I'd be joining The League.

And when had she learned to navigate in four-inch stilettos? There were words for shoes like that and she knew how to draw every ounce of effect from them. Walking or sitting.

I was pretty sure Dad would not have let her leave the house without personal security.

Derek the Dimwit was going to get the shock of his young life when Lynn showed up. He'd be kicking his own ass, which was fine with me. But Ernie, in typical fashion, showed up an hour early, slouched onto the couch and sweated in his new suit until she appeared at the curve of the stairs.

Then unseen forces pulled him to his feet. He was gob struck—left entirely speechless.

Lynn gracefully managed the stairs with an easy step— kick, step— kick, keeping the ruffle of her poppy red gown from tangling around her ankles, and filling the stunned silence with the rustle of silk as her black-gloved fingers trailed soundlessly down the banister. I could tell she was enjoying her entrance way too much. I stepped forward to cover her shoulders with the finely woven shawl she had left draped over the newel post.

This served to break the trance that had overcome Ernie. He fumbled with a clear, florist's package and presented Lynn with one of those bracelet corsages, in blue, which clashed pretty badly with her red dress. Lynn made a quick recovery when she realized she was obligated to wear it, but Ernie caught her brief hesitation and sensed there was a problem. You could see the starch go out of him. Not an auspicious beginning, I thought.

I handed Ernie Lynn's backpack with her change of clothes for the after-grad all-night party. He needed the distraction and something to do with his hands. They left in his father's car, and all I could do was wait for morning and hope for the best.

But at 3:40 am I was jerked from sleep by the sound of a key in the front door — apparently I had dozed off on the living room couch.

I was in the hall by the time the door opened and there stood Lynn. The vamp who had departed hours earlier, draped in high fashion, had reverted to someone I was much more familiar with.

"Lynne? What are you doing home?"

"I hoped you would be in bed."

"What's the matter? Are you crying? Did that idiot Ernie do something?"

"No, no! Not Ernie, I ditched him."

"What do you mean you ditched him? You were supposed to stay together at the after-grad until breakfast was served."

"Oh Lyle! It was so awful. Derek, the Dickhead, brought Hilary . . . can you believe it, Hilary the Harlot . . . to the dance. I couldn't stand it! Derek was all over Hilary like pavement. And she spent her time trying to make sure I didn't miss the road show. So I deeked out around two o'clock with some kids who invited me to a house party."

"Oh, no . . . don't tell me . . ."

"I thought it would be fun but it was awful! I was so shocked when they drove up to that sleazy motel next to the recycling depot. The place is a dump! The room we went into smelled disgusting and the noise level was incredible! There was so much crap going on I didn't know where to look! Younger girls from school were already so drunk when I got there that they were letting boys, letting boys... right in front of everyone!"

She wiped her eyes as if that might clear the picture from her head.

"Some kids were snorting cocaine off the kitchen counter and others were passing joints. Everyone had beer in their hands. Fights were breaking out all around me. A girl was puking on a bedspread and her friends were cheering her on!

"If Dad ever finds out I was there he'll kill me. I had to leave. I worked my way over to the door and . . . Oh God . . . *Ernie* walked in and saw me.

"Oh Lyle, I felt like such a creep. He looked so sad and disappointed in me and not the least bit surprised to see me there. He grabbed my arm and pulled me out the door and over to his dad's car. He opened the car door and waited for me to get in then told me to buckle up and lock my door. His voice was so — dead — and I was so miserable knowing that he knew I had ditched him for such a disgusting orgy.

"I thought about all the math exams he had helped me pr-pr-prepare for. How he always sm- smiles when he sees me. How I l-lied to him and told him you were coming to g-get me because I had a headache but he should stay, and then I sn-sneaked out when he wasn't w-watching."

Her voice ended in a high, squeaky sob. I stood in front of her wishing Mom were here and I was somewhere else, far away — doing guy stuff —while Mom did the stuff she had been in training for, since Lynn was born. Stuff I was completely and purposely unprepared for!

Lynn dragged a used Kleenex from her jacket pocket and blew her nose. This of course gave her a chance to continue her tale of woe.

"We have to present a major French project together on Monday," she wailed, "to our whole class! How am I going to face him?"

Well if there was a positive spin to this whole scenario, it had to be that Derek the Dunderhead was ancient history and my little sister was concerned about the future of an important old friendship.

Lynn sank down onto the hall floor, overcome with tears. Needing a time-out, or succumbing to helplessness, I left her there and dashed across the street to see if I could catch Ernie before he went inside his house.

He was leaning up against an old maple, kicking dejectedly at an exposed root. As I sprinted toward him he pushed away from the tree. He looked as if he was about to call it a night and go in.

"Hey, Ernie, wait up a minute," I called softly.

He turned toward me but said nothing. Wearily, he hunched into his disheveled clothes, head down, hands in his pockets and waited for me to approach.

"Thanks, man," I said. "Thanks for bringing her home. I hate to think what might have happened to her if you hadn't showed up when you did. She's grounded until she leaves for college but you did the right thing. You're a good friend, man. Please don't give up on her now."

Slowly his head came up and he stared at me as if I was more than a little off base.

"Give up on *her*?" he asked. "Seems she has given up on me." He swiped at his nose with one hand and sniffed.

"Nah," I said, "she's in there bawling her eyes out because of the way she treated you when she knows you're the best friend she'll ever have. I've got to get back," I explained. "She pretty much had a breakdown when she got in the door."

I grabbed his hand and shook it until he responded with a decent grip. He lifted his head to look at me. Something changed in his eyes. I think hope entered in. And he became less a boy and more a young man, a pretty decent-looking young man in my opinion.

"I don't usually leave 'em crying," he said with a wry grin. "And tell her *she* gets to present the French project on Monday. I'm merely there to turn the pages of the charts. And she better be well prepared. I need an 'A' in French to get a full scholarship."

I laughed and punched his shoulder. "Give her hell, Ernie."

He turned from me, squaring his shoulders and sauntering toward his parents' house. He lifted a hand in farewell before he went inside.

I walked back to our house and went in, locking up behind me. Lynn was sitting up with her head resting on her raised knees but she seemed to be crying as hard as when I had left her. I watched her search unsuccessfully for another Kleenex. As she eyed the sleeve of her jacket I whipped off my t-shirt and handed it to her.

"Use this. It's easier to wash and you are now in charge of the laundry as well as the cooking, the cleaning, dishes and yard work. But you'll have lots of time. You are grounded until the end of summer!"

Lynn looked up and tried to smile. She eyed the t-shirt, shrugged and used it to blow her nose.

"And no more sniveling! I just gave you the shirt off my back, if you didn't notice." She blew into it again with even more enthusiasm, I thought.

"By the way, Ernie says to get to work on that French project. His scholarship rests on your shoulders. Boy, do you have some fences to mend there. You'll never again be able to walk all over that guy like you've been doing for your whole sorry life."

I saw the beginning of a watery smile challenge her trembling lower lip. "Thanks a lot. As much as I would like to sit here and idolize you, I think I'll just slink off," she said.

I watched her drag herself up and head for the stairs. Thinking back, I believe I did a wise thing when I opted for a fishing trip with my dad and some guys, to celebrate my graduation.

$48.50 !!

By Sheila Blimke

I was jolted awake by a beam of sunshine piercing my eyelids as the sun's rays filtered through tiny perforations in the roll shutters. A quick glance at the bedside clock told me it was 5 am.

A waking dream caused my mind to flash back to a long forgotten, silly incident, which occurred some fifty years ago.

Now fully awake, I lay back on my pillow and began to recall the story. It happened the first year of our marriage. My husband and I, then in our mid- twenties, and living in rental accommodation, had made the decision to set up a stringent savings plan for the purchase of our own house. Both he and I had fairly stable jobs, but salaries back in the fifties were definitely meager, thus finances had to be handled with extreme care. We had determined never to dip into "the mortgage fund," consequently, our budget covering essentials was extremely tight. Entertainment funds practically non-existent.

It so happened, the year of our marriage, our local community desperately needed to replace its outdoor hockey rink, in order to provide the local youngsters with a place to gather and hone their skating skills. Such a recreational site was deemed essential for the children to expend their energy, in a safe, inexpensive and enjoyable environment.

In order to raise funds for the venture, it was decided to begin by holding a Box Social and Dance at the local schoolhouse. This entailed recruiting, for a very nominal fee, any local reasonably talented musicians to provide dance music. Funds for the skating rink would be raised from the sale of box lunches provided by the women in the district. Each lady would prepare a lunch for two, place it in a fancy, decorated box to be held aloft by the volunteer auctioneer, then bid on by the men in attendance. The successful bidder had, as his reward, the pleasure of eating lunch with whichever lady prepared the box. Of course, all the married men knew better than to be the final bidder on any box other than the one prepared by his own wife!

On the evening of the Social, just as my box was held high for the bidding to begin, the schoolhouse door burst open and in lunged a huge, grubby, more than slightly inebriated stranger. Apparently, he had been on his way home from the local pub, when he noticed the array of vehicles parked at the schoolhouse and decided to join the party. When the auctioneer signaled the bidding on my box to begin, the fellow bellowed out, "Five Bucks!"

All eyes turned to the stranger since his bid was so unexpected. Usually the bidding started at one dollar and slowly inched upward, almost never surpassing five dollars. In desperation my eyes searched the hall for my husband, who, apparently, had slipped outside for a cigarette. Immediately, some of the craftier fellows present decided this might be a fine opportunity to increase the funds for the rink and began bidding against the newcomer.

"$5.50!" shouted our neighbour.

"$6.00" bellowed the stranger, weaving unsteadily on his feet.

And on it went, back and forth, now inching up by 25- or 50-cent bids. By now I am in an agony of worry trying to locate my husband to get me out of having to eat lunch with this obnoxious, inebriated big spender. The bidding had now reached $8.00. I am in a panic, with still no sign of my husband. Suddenly the door burst open, and in he flew, up to the foot of the stage yelling, "$48.50! I bid $48.50!"

The auctioneer slammed down his hammer, a look of astonishment on his face and yelled, "Sold!" then quickly reached for the next box.

My feelings of relief at being rescued evaporated quickly, turning to shock, as thoughts of our stringent budget sprang to mind and realization of the consequences of my husband's rash act sank in.

"The bid had only reached $8.00," I said, gazing at my beleaguered husband as we sat together, choking down what now had obviously become a gold-plated lunch. "What on earth possessed you to bid so high?"

My husband's face blanched as he stared at me in dismay. "Good Lord!" he said. "When Tom rushed out to tell me I had better get in quick because some drunk was bidding on your lunch box, he must have said the bid was already up *FOR $8.00*. I thought he said, 'FORTY-EIGHT dollars!'"

As long as I can remember, that newly erected skating complex was known by all the locals as the $48.50 Rink!

Famous Last Step

By Jody Chadderton

How to share the splendour
of a postcard vista
with loved ones worlds away
— a photograph?
Is that what you felt,
the need to share,
when you parked your car,
stepped over the barricade
camera in hand
to capture a moment?

What happened on that ledge?
This is how I see it:
you raise your camera and —
the beauty! — more wondrous still
framed in the lens —
bowls you over.

Is it too horrific to wonder:
did you squeeze the shutter?
And how did it feel,
that first step onto —
nothing?

Do Not Take Me Away

By Sally Swedburg

Nurse Evie Bacon lay helpless on her bed in the small, one-window bedroom of her spacious mission home. Her home was on a little hill up a path from Curran Memorial Hospital in Zorzor, Liberia, West Africa. There were other much larger bedrooms in the house, but Evie chose this small room so that patients from the overflowing mission hospital could occupy the other bedrooms. Evie's main concern was always for the patients. She cared little about herself and her own needs.

Now, for the first time in thirty-five years of missionary service, fifty-five-year-old Evie knew that she was the one who was very ill. And she had to have others take care of her. Her role had shifted and she didn't like it at all. She desperately wanted to get up and nurse her patients as she always had—even when she was ill herself. Having malaria, dysentery or worms had never kept her in bed for more than a day. Often she would be seen hurrying from one patient to another looking pale and tired, and everyone knew she needed nursing herself. But somehow or other, she always seemed to recover quickly, except for this time.

Evie had lain in bed for almost a week but it seemed like an eternity to her. She just wasn't getting any better, and Doctor Carl Martin, the missionary doctor in Zorzor, wasn't answering her questions.

"Too early to tell what you've got. You'll have to have more blood tests," was all he would say. This really irritated her because she was sure he knew what was wrong. However, she was too weak and sick to show her anger like she usually did when he or one of the staff aggravated her. Evie's quick temper was her only character flaw. She was sometimes difficult to work with, but she was an excellent nurse and everyone knew it.

Doctor Carl had often tried to cheer her up. He distorted his face in a comical way to get a rise out of her, but she could barely manage a smile. If anyone could make her laugh or make her angry, it was Carl. And although Carl both angered and amused her, on this day she could express neither emotion. She was simply too weak and too frightened to say more than, "Oh God, what is wrong with me?" and close her eyes. Sometimes God seemed far away.

At the end of that seemingly endless week, a week of exceptionally hot and sultry weather, Dr. Carl came by to tell Evie that the mission plane was coming soon to take her to Phebe Hospital. It was a large and better-equipped hospital that specialized in caring for critically-ill patients. The hospital was eighty miles away in central Liberia.

"Evie, I'm sure you'll agree with me that the best place for you now is Phebe. You'll get even better help down there. I don't need to tell you that. And you'll be back with us before you know it. The plane is coming later this afternoon to pick you up."

Carl noticed how hard Evie was trying to respond to this news; he also noticed a look of anguish cross her face as a dark cloud quickly crosses the surface of the moon. He knew she realized how serious her illness was.

As Carl looked at Evie, he saw that her eyes were wet with tears. Evie had never cried in front of others, although she came very close to it whenever one of her patients died. Carl sensed her agony and said with more compassion than he'd ever felt toward Evie, "Would you like me to pray with you, Evie?"

She looked at him realizing that he had never prayed with her before; his voice sounded so different—loving and kind. "Yes, I'd like that." Her voice sounded different too—weak, hesitant, feeble, like an elderly lady who'd had a stroke.

Carl didn't often pray with his patients but the words seemed to flow easily for him this day: "Dear God, I come to you in behalf of Evie. You know how much she needs You and Your healing. Strengthen her and give her hope. Help her to trust in You, and to remember Your promise to work for the good of those who love You. And You know Dear God, that Evie loves You; we thank You for everything you've done for her and all that You are going to do to help her. In Jesus' name, Amen."

Carl glanced up at Evie as he finished the prayer. She had turned her head away trying to hide her weeping. He thought he'd better leave before he embarrassed her.

"I'll have Diane stop by and pack a suitcase for you. And I'll come to get you when the plane arrives. You'll be in better hands soon. See you later."

During her illness Evie saw few of her friends. The only people who were allowed to see her were gowned and masked hospital staff and the missionary pastor. Carl had good reasons for this isolation since he suspected that this particular illness was contagious.

Evie had plenty of time to think about her Liberian life. She remembered the good times which had been many, and the not so good times too. She had often given her last penny or change of clothes to the Liberians. And still she didn't think she'd had any needs that had not been met—except for right now. She knew what people at the mission station thought of her. They had often scolded her for her hit and miss eating and sleeping habits, her long hours at the hospital and the low priority she gave to socializing or simply relaxing. They were always concerned about her health and welfare which she thought completely unnecessary. She did not think her actions were unusual but essential for the work that God had called her to do. In fact, they had been wonderful years doing what she had always dreamed of doing as a young girl growing up in Sioux City, Iowa.

She remembered the earlier years in Liberia as being more difficult. She had had to travel by horse or by foot into the villages to deliver babies and to minister to the sick. After the mission hospital was built, many people from remote villages were reluctant to come there for treatment at first. But as word of mouth spread about all the good treatment that people received at the hospital, more and more people started coming. This meant that the medical staff had to travel less into the villages. Soon horses weren't used at all when four-wheel drive vehicles and mission planes became available and new roads and airfields were constructed.

Yes, Evie pondered, many changes had taken place through the years and God had been so good to her and to her Liberian friends. Why then, had this happened to her? Her friends needed her so much and she couldn't help them. Her prayers seemed to go unanswered. She just didn't understand!

Suddenly, she thought of Taizu—and a faint glimmer of hope shone through her despondency as a rainbow appears after a rainstorm. Taizu seemed to be recovering. And Taizu's symptoms and treatment were almost the same as hers. She had wondered for awhile if this young pregnant woman would pull through and it looked as if she had!

Before Evie got sick, she had nursed Taizu day and night for 2 weeks, seldom leaving her side. Evie remembered how Taizu had pleaded with her when she first arrived in the hospital: Mama Bacon, (Mama was a Loma title of respect), you must save my life and the life of my baby because there's no one besides me to take care of her. The father doesn't want to have anything to do with me or the baby and my relatives won't help me because I'm not married. Please ask God to make me well!"

Evie knew that in Liberia both boys and girls went to school, but boys were expected to continue with their education, no matter what, while girls would have to quit school if they became pregnant. Most of the time, the girls would be fully responsible for taking care of their babies since the relatives considered that they were to blame for their pregnancies. It was not easy for a young girl to raise a child on her own.

As she nursed Taizu, Doctor Carl's wife, Denise, admonished, "Evie, if you don't eat properly and get some sleep, you're going to die an early death and then what good will you be to anyone?"

Now the fear of death permeated her heart and mind. She felt chilled and started trembling. She knew she had to get hold of herself and stop thinking such morbid thoughts. I'm not going to die and I'm not going on that plane to Phebe! She knew that many patients taken from Curran Hospital to Phebe never came back. No, she would not let them take her away! Even though she prepared to defy Doctor Carl and insist on being treated where she was, she knew there was little she could do but protest her removal to Phebe.

Just as she was planning her last ditch plea to be cared for where she was, Diane, one of the missionary nurses, came into the room. Evie liked Diane—maybe she would see things her way.

"Hi Evie," Diane said. "How ya doin? It won't be long now before you'll be on the mend, once you get down to Phebe."

"I'm not going to Phebe. Tell Carl to call the pilot and tell him not to come. I don't need to go to Phebe. I can get well here just as fast. All I need is TLC."

Her voice was whispery and weak. Her attempts to sound strong and convincing failed.

Diane responded with patience and love as she began packing Evie's suitcase. "I can only imagine how hard it must be for you, Evie, but you know as well as I do, that we don't have the equipment here to give you all the tests which you need. They'll determine what you have and then give you the best treatment available. You'll see—everything will work out and you'll be back soon. God always knows what's best for us, right?"

"I know, I know," Evie replied in her thready voice, "but why can't I stay here like Taizu did? She didn't have a lot of tests and she had similar symptoms to me. And she recovered in this hospital." She felt drained and despondent as if she were a runner who had given it her best but lost the race.

Diane could see Evie was exhausted and needed to sleep. She spoke softly to Evie, saying, "It was only because of your excellent care and God's grace that Taizu recovered. She would have benefited from being at Phebe also. Now try and get some sleep and you'll feel stronger when you wake up. I'll finish this packing and be back in about an hour."

Before leaving, Diane glanced at Evie. She had fallen into a deep sleep with a peaceful expression on her pale, drawn face.

Diane walked slowly down the hill on the path through some of the majestic, tropical trees—huge cottonwoods, stately coconut palms and the lavish, flame red flamboyant. She hardly noticed the beauty around her as she wondered about Evie's mysterious disease and what the future would hold for Evie. She looked up and a breath of a prayer floated up to the heavens.

The sound of an airplane had awakened Evie. Her heart sank, knowing what it meant. She was not happy when Carl, Diane and a few Liberian nurses came into her room with a stretcher and some clean sheets.

"Evie," said Carl, "we're going to put you on the stretcher now and take you out to the plane. Just try and relax and pretend you're going to the Canary Islands." The only holidays Evie had ever taken had been to the Canary Islands—not too far from Liberia. She'd enjoyed them for the brief reprieve from her medical and missionary challenges, but was always anxious to get back.

The stretcher bearers carried her carefully through the hospital and out onto the runway. That's when Evie made one more attempt to remain in Curran Hospital. She cried out with laboured breathing, "Please, please! Don't let them take me away!" She hoped that her Liberian friends, who were standing nearby and watching, would intervene. She hoped they would come and get her and convince the doctor not to do this. But not one of them came. Instead they waved goodbye and cried as she was lifted into the plane and it took off.

Two weeks later, Evie died of Lassa fever. The disease had been diagnosed too late for any treatment to be effective. She returned to Zorzor as she had intuited: in a wooden box. The hospital staff removed the box from the plane and reverently took it to the grave site. They lowered the box into the deep hole. The staff then took off their hospital coveralls and masks and threw them on top of the wooden box as they'd been instructed. Lassa fever was contagious.

When the service took place the day Evie was laid to rest, the mourners had to stand 10 feet away from the grave site. She had been buried so fast and unceremoniously that hardly anyone knew what was happening—especially the Liberians. The missionary chaplain at the High School and the Bishop of the Lutheran Church had a few words to say. But the Liberians didn't really understand why they were not allowed to throw themselves on the grave of their good friend, Evie, or why there was little pomp and ceremony. They talked and cried among themselves, "Bacca, Bacca," (their name for Evie), "What's happening. Why don't they let us see you and get close to you? We don't understand it. We loved you so much. You were like one of us. Can't they see we have to show our love for you?"

The women tried to break through the rope barriers around the grave site in order to throw themselves on the grave but they were held back. The hospital staff explained how contagious the illness was in several Liberian languages. Although they quieted down, nothing could be said to satisfy them completely.

Two weeks later a memorial service of great pomp and ceremony was held in the church in Zorzor. Evie would have preferred the simple grave side service but her Liberian friends wanted to show their love and sorrow in the Liberian way. Although they couldn't throw themselves on top of the grave site as was their custom, the two-hour service made them happy. All the mourners who attended the memorial service felt Evie had been suitably honoured at last.

Evie had finally come HOME. To this day, there stands a memorial grave stone by the hospital in Zorzor in memory of the Florence Nightingale of Liberia—Evie Bacon.

Paper Girl

By Sue Whittaker

They called me "the paper girl" when I rang the bell and announced I was collecting for *Star Weekly*. What a scramble that would set in motion! Trying to locate the 64 cents they owed at the end of each month was a struggle for many housewives. And what an insight into human nature for a ten-year-old girl. While I was welcomed three weeks out of the month for delivering the main source of family entertainment for the evening, on that fourth Wednesday, the looks were tinged with coldness—even suspicion.

"Is it that time — again?" several housewives on my route would exclaim as they rolled their eyes, then left me standing under a dripping eave, facing a closed door, while they raided their milk money or their children's piggy banks to turn the wolf from the door.

Or one of my school mates would answer the door. "Mom!" she would yell, "it's the paper girl. She wants money!" One short hour ago we had been on a first name basis. Now I was a drain on the family resources with no particular identity.

"Paper girl," I would snort inwardly as I slung my heavy bag over my shoulder and trudged on to the next drop. More like "muscle and bone girl" or "dedicated delivery girl" or "neither snow, nor rain nor heat girl." A paper girl would not have made it through the first week of deliveries. She would have been shredded and eaten up by the first dog that challenged her at the garden gate. A paper girl would have caved under the weight of those forty Star Weeklies, dried up and blown away in the heat of the summer sun or have perished in the winter cold. I was no paper girl. I was a young entrepreneur with financial responsibilities and a daunting task to perform once a week.

You learned something else about human nature on a paper route. It wasn't necessarily the poorest of your clients who came up 64 cents short on the last Wednesday of the month. "Come back on Saturday," I'd be told by many who had new cars in the driveway and the blue light of a television flickering through the living room window. And when you did, you might find no car in the driveway and get no response from repeated knocking or ringing. It put a kid off. If my own mother had not been as financially strapped as she was, I would probably have had far less forbearance with the runaround. But I certainly knew better than to protest or demand.

For me, the rewards of that paper route had little to do with the paltry return on investment. My joy came in the pride and sense of ownership I took in the actual publication itself. After all, I was an important link between publication and readership. If I didn't hustle on a Wednesday afternoon, all the rest was for naught.

So I read each edition from front to back. I learned about this great country I was growing up in and got my first insight into what other Canadian provinces looked like. I experienced some sense of big city life in Canada. The movies offered nothing like the *Star Weekly*. The movies were from Hollywood and seldom touched down in Canada. The books we read were largely English in origin. But the *Star Weekly* managed to get camera men into Vancouver, Calgary, Toronto or Ottawa when new buildings went up, the Queen visited Canada or a Prime Minister was sworn in. I saw colour photos of hockey players, actors, singers, politicians and Governors- General.

None of those, however, made it on to my bedroom walls. It was the weekly shot of the big Hollywood stars that spurred me into my first frenzy of interior decoration. Doris Day, Rock Hudson, Dinah Shore, Elvis Presley and Debbie Reynolds all found a place from which to display those million dollar smiles.

They were the last faces I saw before I fell asleep and the heavenly host that greeted me when I woke up. The Hollywood Room was my favourite place— by far —to lollygag in those days.

The *Star Weekly* got me through school projects with pictures and information I would otherwise have been unable to access. Before printers and scanners, if you didn't have the original copy you were right out of luck. It often made my night job, baby sitting, more bearable in the days before televisions were in widespread use and radio stations were all "am" and static was endemic.

The large coloured comic section exposed me to Al Capp's *L'il Abner* and the rest of the Dogpatchers, *Pogo* and the denizens of the swamp, as well as that sterling hero, Prince Valiant. It was instrumental in developing my sense of humour (Heart o' Oak, Eat your front porch) and opened my eyes to the world of wildlife painting with the beautiful watercolours of birds by Victoria's, J. Fenwick Lansdowne.

I read about prairie farmers and saw them on their land, I followed east coast fishermen to the Grand Banks, and I saw the lighthouse at Peggy's Cove long before I was able to cross Canada in 1972. I was already a fan of CBC Radio, continuing to develop the sense of country I had come to cherish, by the time the *Star Weekly* ceased publishing in the 1960's.

Regardless of the lifelong skeletal implications, lugging forty pounds of papers around the entire downtown section of Kaslo was a character building challenge that shaped a paper girl into a woman of some strength.

<u>Autumn, Winter and Uh, Oh!</u>

By Allene Halliday

My sister Elaine shimmers in
vibrant green, luminous gold,
sizzling orange and
radiant periwinkle.

My sister Pat is stunning in
carnation red, glacial white,
sable black and sapphire blue.

Clearly, fashion's colour spectrum
for Elaine is Autumn's;
and for Pat it is
undoubtedly Winter's.

But what is mine?

I used to sparkle in
spring shades of sunny coral,
Aegean aqua, luscious cream
and tantalizing kiwi.

Now, my wardrobe's hues lean toward
woodsy taupe, pale jonquil,
cool lime and crisp watermelon.

What's going on?

Whether I like it or not,
gray hair is
shoving me
into the shades of Summer.

April Fools

By Maureen Kresfelder

"Look at that huge spider!"
I said, my eyes agog,
my voice a screech.
I pointed to the hassock
cradling my favourite aunt's feet.
My aunt leapt up —
"Where is it, where is it?" she cried,
as her eyes frantically swept the area.
"April Fools!" I said, smiling gleefully.
But my 9-year-old smile faded
as she reached over
and grabbed my shoulders
and looked me in the eye.
"We are not amused,"
she said like a long-ago queen.
"Don't ever, ever, do that again.
I am nobody's fool and don't you forget it!"
And I never have.

Pretty Dresses

By Jody Chadderton

Remember all the sewing you did for the three of us when we were kids? First one little girl with a pretty little dress made by her mom's own loving hands. Then two little girls dressed alike in pretty little dresses made by their mom's own loving hands. "Are they twins?" strangers sometimes asked, seeing the identical dresses but oblivious to the difference in size.

"Yes they are," Mom wants to answer. "Anne is three and a half and Jo is almost two."

Finally, three little girls dressed all the same in pretty dresses made by their mom's own loving hands. No, not a single person asked if they were triplets. Three Christmas dresses, three Easter suits, three summer shifts, three dressing gowns, three school jumpers, all lovingly made by Mom.

Mary Poppins dresses we called the rose and white checked dresses with hidden snaps up the back and full gathered skirts. Why did we call them Mary Poppins dresses? Mary herself wouldn't wear something that frilly, but perhaps her young charge, Jane Banks, had a dress like that.

Several years later the largest dress would be recycled as Jill's Centennial dress. Everyone in 1967 had a special dress representative of a time 100 years before. Jill wore the Mary Poppins dress remade with an extra row or two of eyelet lace at the hem and long white bloomers underneath. I can't remember if she wore a hat, but I know Anne and I did. We wore bonnets and new dresses, again made by Mom. Anne's was chocolate brown calico and mine was navy. They had high waists and soft gathers. The matching bonnets had lace trim and long ribbons we could tie under our chins to one side or the other.

My very favourite of our identical dresses were what we called our Polly Anna dresses. They were in dark subdued colours: wine, navy, gold and brown. They had high lace-trimmed collars and long gathered sleeves with lace-trimmed cuffs. Soft gathers fell from the dropped waist and a wide navy satin sash was tied in a perfect bow at the back.

I remember wearing our dresses to church, so proud of our lovely new dresses and the perfect bows. But these were our Christmas dresses, meaning it was wintertime, and although the fabric was in wintry colours it was a fine cotton and our church was old, poorly insulated and inadequately heated. We tried taking our coats off, but we gave up and stayed bundled in our coats, our prettiest dresses ever hidden from view.

They wouldn't stay hidden through the whole service though. We three whispered conspiratorially, then removed our coats just before communion. I was the one to handle the timing. One thing I loved about the Anglican church was the predictability. I had memorized all the important stuff: when to stand, kneel, sit, bow, when to reach for the prayer book and when to grab the hymnal, the colours of the minister's robe — white for Christmas and Easter, purple for Lent, green for Epiphany. I knew just when to get our money out for collection and, most important of all, when to take off our coats in order to show off our brand new Polly Anna Christmas dresses for a walk down the aisle to receive a blessing from Canon Yerbourgh.

Looking Out for Shirley

By Maureen Olsen

My work involves frequent trips to the east side of Vancouver. I park at a distance from my destination so I can walk through the depressed area with its littered streets: cast off Styrofoam cups, discarded fast food containers, used needles. It helps keep me aware of the conditions there. These trips are not comfortable; they cause me to feel apprehensive and guilty. Yes, guilty, because I know a daughter of one of my close friends is known to live and work here. Have I ever looked for her? No. Would I recognize her if I saw her? I doubt it, but I remember her black wavy hair and the way she tilted her head.

After all, it's been about ten years since I last saw her, and her parents certainly haven't shared any pictures they might have received. They tell me when they hear from her, but they haven't said anything for over a year.

I usually wear a business suit, brogues, a Tilley hat, and carry a raincoat with me. I choose to walk down the narrow sidewalks of the less traffic-congested streets, dark with shadows. I keep to the edge of the curb so I won't need to step over some vagrant's legs protruding into the sidewalk. I try not to look into recessed doorways because I don't want to see who might be there. The smells of urine and vomit are not as stifling in the winter, but in the summer are often gagging.

I've started to carry coins in my pocket in case I encounter a person who might be able to use a small donation offered discretely. It is fair to say that I walk briskly along to try to reach my goal as quickly as possible, complete my business, and return to my car.

Recently, my friend, Bill, phoned me to tell me he had heard from his daughter, Shirley. She was living in a room on Drake Street. She thought she would try to come home for a visit, but not immediately. He said she sounded sad.

Later that week I was called down to the east side. I certainly wasn't looking for her. But there she was.

"Shirley?" I quietly said to the young woman sitting in a doorway. She was very thin, her arms were almost skeletal. Her dress was soiled and draped loosely about her. She still had some curl in her black hair which hung about her face. She tilted her head in the way I remembered as she looked up. She answered hesitantly.

"Yes, whaddya want?"

"Nothing, your dad, Bill, said you were in this area. I didn't expect to recognize you."

"Well now you've seen me, whaddya want?" she whispered.

Startled, I replied, "What would you like me to do? Tell him I saw you?"

"No, I'm not ready. I don't want them to know."

"Will I see you again?" I asked.

"I don't know how long I'll be staying here. I have to keep moving."

As I reached into my pocket for some bills, I said, "Take care. I hope you'll be safe." I passed the money to her as quickly as I could and then continued on my way without looking back. I didn't tell her parents.

Over the ensuing months I looked for her. I traversed my route on the lookout, hoping to see Shirley again. She had been in my thoughts. I slowed my pace to enable me to look around. To my great surprise a quiet voice said, "Dave?"

I stopped, amazed, looking around to see who had spoken. A skeletal female leaned up against a door in a recessed area. There was another woman with her, half holding her up. They shivered in their ragged clothes. Shirley introduced me to her friend, Mary, who was propping her up.

"I've been watching for you. It's been a long time. You've lost weight," I said.

"Some of us have been away at a farm. Mary and I decided to come back to town. We feel safer here." Her voice was weak. Her words came slowly.

"You're together then. Are you getting by?"

"Sometimes," Mary said.

"Here, let me give you something. What else can I do?" I gave her some bills from my pocket.

"Nothing. This will help," Shirley said as she looked away from me. "I still can't face going home."

I nodded. "I know they want to see you. Here's my card if you ever want to get hold of me."

I carried on my way, feeling distressed and helpless. I would have scooped her up and taken her home if I could.

A change in responsibilities kept me away from the area for six months. As I parked my car I recalled my last contact with Shirley. I really didn't expect to see her. Once again I walked my usual route. About a block away from the last place I had spoken with her, a woman was walking towards me. When she was almost passed, she grabbed my sleeve.

"I know you. You're Shirley's friend."

"How is she?" I asked.

"She's gone. Her body was found last week. I miss her so much!" she sniffled.

Before I could say anything she disappeared through a doorway.

No Love Lost

By Sue Whittaker

Corporal Jefferies was reporting on the state of the traveling public to the dispatcher, Mandy, back at the station. He had decided to turn around and return to patrol duty when a car went by him like a bat out of hell.

"Oh, got a lady in a big hurry. I'm in pursuit!" he informed Dispatch.

Having the road to himself, he spun the cruiser in a circle, turned on his flashing light and went flat out in an effort to identify the license number of the red Toyota Celica eating up the road ahead of him.

The siren did it. The car slowed down and pulled over to the side of the road. Approaching from behind, he could see that the driver appeared to be searching for her driver's license and registration. Her window was down.

"Good morning, ma'am," he said, as she thrust a handful of identification at him. "I just clocked you at 120 kilometers an hour."

"That's because I had to go twice the speed limit to make up for the time I lost following those idiot geezers, who should be banned from the road during business hours," she snarled.

Oh! Some attitude here, he thought. "Well, now you're going to be even later and also somewhat poorer after paying this," he informed her, handing her the ticket he had filled out.

"But this is the maximum!" she protested.

"Yeh," he said, "everybody else was so law-abiding this morning, I have to make my quota on you alone. You have a good day ma'am. And if I may say, you should leave a little earlier tomorrow morning." Try as he might, he was unable to control the smirk that spread across his face.

"Thank you, Officer. With advice like that you are sure to become head of the detachment."

"I am head of the detachment, but thank you for your insight," he said and sauntered back to his cruiser.

That morning's conversation was running through his head when a shopping cart whipped by him as he was picking up some groceries later that day. The edge of the cart clipped his basket, tipping it and sending oranges, apples and lemons rolling across the floor of the supermarket. At the same time, a glass bottle of salad dressing hit the floor and smashed at his feet. His shoes and pants were covered in oily goop.

And didn't that spiky hair look familiar?

She stopped and looked back as the noise registered. If that smug assessment meant anything, he figured she'd ID'ed him, too.

"Nice hair," he said, "does your lawn boy moonlight?"

"Hey, you're looking a little folically challenged, yourself. Most of your barber's bill must be in the nature of a finder's fee."

He laughed. "You've got me there. I've been shaving my head for so long it's forgotten one of its functions."

"Only one?" Her left eyebrow rose sharply.

"Your point," he conceded with a grimace.

"Well, I'd love to stay and help you clean up, but I'm a little behind schedule today — due to a highwayman, masquerading as a bureaucratic zealot whom I ran afoul of this morning."

She started to move on, then stopped and turned back to him. "Oh, if they charge you for breakage, you just remember, 'what goes around, comes around.'"

And she was off.

"Set your alarm earlier tonight," he called after her.

She didn't reply verbally, but that was a very naughty gesture she displayed over her shoulder as she flounced away.

He shook his head. Maggie hadn't changed a bit since high school.

Paradise Lost

By Jody Chadderton

Billie Leone tossed her gardening gloves on the top stair of her front porch. Then, removing her sombrero to fan her face, Billie tucked a damp wisp of white hair behind her ear and flopped down on the stair to rest. It wasn't actually a sombrero, just a weathered straw hat, but she liked to amuse herself with what few Spanish words she knew while she was at her San Carlos casa. "Mi casa, su casa," she used to say when she had visitors, back before the terrorist attack made crossing borders difficult, when tourists still visited, when the Club Med still operated, when the air strip buzzed with private planes, the rich and famous flitting from one playground to the next. They will be back, Billie predicted, gazing at the stretch of white beach, strangely deserted under a clear blue sky. I came back as I have done every year, drawn to the beaches and the waves and the mountain above the village, Tetas de Cabra, goat teats, they called it. Of course it was upside down, and she tried once again to picture a goat lying on its back. But the teats would not point straight skyward like that, would they? She had returned after 9/11 as she had returned after Victor's death, surprising friends and relatives with her determination to carry on as before. And now she once again covered her white hair with her sombrero and shook her gloves as she stood. "I must ask Rosa 'como se dice gloves en espanol?'"

Painting Winter

By Jody Chadderton

Let's paint a picture in ice cream
–vanilla, of course.
With scoops of maple-walnut
piled up on both sides of the road
which should be darker,
maybe chocolate with a fresh dusting
of something white,
something like coconut or icing sugar
only colder.
The rest, beyond the banks,
is white too. Dollops of whipped cream
and marshmallow topping
and clouds of meringue
and constant sprinkles from above.
Keep the picture cold
for just awhile.
Now let's paint a picture
of something green.

The Stranger

By Sheila Blimke

Comfortably seated under a shady patio umbrella at our favorite deli, my best friend, Karen, and I laughed helplessly as we waited for our lunch to arrive, reliving the tirade just heaped upon us by our tennis instructor. On a whim, we had decided to enroll in advanced tennis lessens at our local club, unfortunately forgetting we just might not be at the appropriate physical level before embarking on such a project. We soon realized our mistake after several pointed remarks by our lean, muscled and highly egotistical tennis pro. As we sat weighing our options on how to gracefully withdraw from his program, a young woman stepped out from the deli into the patio. Her eyes searched the crowd, then suddenly she turned in our direction and, approaching our table, said in a relieved voice,

"Thank goodness, a familiar face! There isn't a vacant table left. Do you mind if I join you?"

"Not at all," we both said, surprised, as she quickly pulled out a chair and seated herself. Obviously, she must be Karen's friend since I didn't know her. I waited for Karen to introduce us, but she remained silent. After catching her breath the woman glanced at me and said, "How is Paula? I haven't seen her in months."

Confused, I replied, "Paula?"

The woman suddenly looked closely at me, gasped and said, "Aren't you Meg Lane, Paula Greer's sister?"

"No, I'm afraid not," I replied.

Now, utterly flustered, the woman grasped her purse and stood up.

"I'm so sorry!" she said. "I met Meg only once but I was sure you were she! Please excuse me!"

Obviously mortified, she turned and fled from the patio.

It all happened so quickly, Karen and I sat speechless, finally regaining our wits as the waiter arrived with lunch. The episode jogged my memory, reminding me of a somewhat similar incident that had occurred in my father's life. As we lingered over lunch, I told Karen the story.

"My father grew up in a small town in England, adjacent to a busy seaport on the shores of the North Sea. The port, though deemed off limits to the children, became a natural magnet to the young boys. My dad was the middle child in a large happy family; however, this tranquility came to an abrupt end the year he turned seventeen. His mother contracted a serious disease and within a few short weeks succumbed to her illness. His father was a man of few words, often referred to by locals as 'the quietest man in the port'; the mother, on the other hand, had been vivacious and jolly, always the center of the household. Now, without her as its nucleus, and the father being of such a remote temperament, the family seemed to lose its focal point. This loss was devastating to the younger children. Struggling to adjust as best they could, the family carried on, some striking out on their own, others marrying and moving away. The remaining members stayed on in the family home.

"As was the custom at that time, men still congregated at the local men's club. One evening, my dad's older brother, Tom, was swapping tales with his friends when a big, strapping stranger walked into the club. After taking a good long look about the room, he came over to Tom's table and seated himself. Tom and his companions nodded an acknowledgement and continued on with their discussion. The stranger remained at their table, calmly drinking his ale, seemingly content to sit quietly listening to the conversation. Eventually he rose, nodded to those still seated, and left. On his departure Tom inquired of the others, 'Who was that chap?'

"But no one seemed to know.

"When the club closed a few minutes later, Tom made his way home. My dad, along with one of his brothers and their father were all there when Tom arrived. To his surprise, seated in a chair in the corner, was none other than the stranger who had been at the club. No introduction was made when Tom entered so he approached his father and whispered, 'Who is that fellow?'

"'I don't know!' said his father, 'We thought he was a friend of yours!'

"Just then, Sam, their ancient family dog, pushed his way through the door, hesitating a moment, his rheumy old eyes surveying the scene. Suddenly, he made an attempt to lunge at the stranger, his wobbly old legs propelling him as far as the man's feet. There he collapsed, whimpering. The stranger knelt and began scratching behind the dog's ears. The animal raised his head in a feeble attempt to lick the man's face.

"'Good God!' cried the father, bolting from his chair. 'He's your brother Frank! Come back from the dead!!'

"Frank, the youngest boy, still a child when his mother died, found it extremely difficult coping with life without her. Attempting to fill this void he began spending much of his spare time down at the docks watching the ships jostle about in the seaport, regularly being threatened and chased home by the dockhands. Then one day, barely into his teens, he simply disappeared. The father did all in his power to trace his son with no success. Finally, as the months went by with no sign of the missing child, the family was forced to accept the fact he would no longer be with them. The only plausible explanation: he had fallen from the docks, and his body washed out to sea.

"In fact, the boy, by lying about his age, had somehow managed to talk his way into being taken on as a cabin boy on a merchant ship destined for China. There he spent the next ten years of his life, making no contact with his home or family until the day he reappeared at the club. He left a small scrawny boy, to return a big burly seaman.

"And the only one to recognize him was Sam — their old family dog."

The Knickers Epiphany

By Sue Whittaker

"Well, that was awfully nice of Eileen and Bob to have the whole head table over for drinks before the banquet, wasn't it?"

Mazie's husband grunted in reply as their car wound its way around the lake to the Community Hall. "Humph. Look at this area," he complained. "I am so glad we settled on the lower part of Falling Lake. Can you imagine living this close to our neighbours? I'd be dead in a week — from self-inflicted wounds — if not natural causes. Rats in a warren have more space than this."

"Don't get yourself all worked up," advised Mazie. "You have to do your Retiring Chair thing with some dignity. Just remember to shake hands and smile like a schmuck. In a few hours your life will be your own again. You can hang in there for that long."

The look he gave her made her wonder if that was indeed going to be possible.

"Come on, Mr. Chair," she teased, giving him a gentle poke in the ribs, "I promise to make it worth your while."

Hugh looked over at her and broke out in a big grin. "You think that is always going to work with me?"

"'Til hell freezes over is my guess," she replied. "Here we are. The piper is pacing, ready to go. Kiss for good luck?" Mazie asked, leaning over towards him. He took her jaw in his long, work-roughened fingers and pressed his lips tenderly against her own. As she opened her eyes he winked at her.

"Stay close, Maze," he growled. "I'll get your door." He turned off the engine, got out, then started around the car toward her.

They entered the hall, hand in hand, with Mazie on Hugh's right. Following close behind the piper, they were enveloped in the strains of *Scotland the Brave*. They approached the tables situated in a semi-circle around the dance floor over which they were walking. The guests rose from their seats to applaud warmly in appreciation of Hugh's twelve years as Chair of the company they all depended on for a living. And it had been a good living because of his leadership. TeckCo profits had soared and so had employee fortunes under a profit-sharing program he had introduced and shepherded along.

One particularly well-oiled guest reached across Mazie to shake Hugh's hand, separating the couple and knocking Mazie off-balance. As she rocked backwards, one high heel caught a splash of wine someone had spilled on the way to the tables. Tipping backwards, she was unable to regain her equilibrium. Then, the errant foot of another woman stepping to the side to avoid a collision with Mazie's windmilling arms, destabilized her even farther. That was enough to send her feet up in the air and land her flat on her back which wouldn't have been so bad if her legs hadn't continued in their backwards motion settling her knees on either side of her ears. Unfortunately, the filmy skirts of her flowered gray dress did not follow suit.

While the piper continued on course, unaware of the scuffle behind him, the guests in the area of Mazie's fall from grace were stunned by the spectacle of the upended Mazie but even more so by the revelation therein. For Mazie, it seemed, while demure in her outer dress, was rather fond of flashy lingerie: expensive red undergarments, made of satin, high-cut in the French style, involving an elaborate garter belt and silky stockings.

As Hugh disengaged from the meaty hand of his well-wisher and cast an eye backwards, he saw only the final flourish of his wife's incomplete backwards flip. Turning to rush to her aid, he became tangled in the melee behind him. Mazie was not moving a muscle having been winded by the force of her fall, so by the time

Hugh reached her side she had been on view for an agonizingly long number of moments.

"You okay?" he whispered as he knelt down and bent towards her ear. He slid one hand under her neck to help ease her up.

"Yes, and you will be too if you get me out of here fast!" she wheezed, rolling up to a sitting position whilst easing her legs down to the floor and straightening her dress.

"Put your arms around my neck," he said as he slipped one arm under her knees and the other under her shoulders. He pushed to his feet, nodded to his Vice Chair, Charlie Burns, to take over, and carried his wife out to their car. Stunned silence had exploded into noise and uneasy, choked laughter behind them.

"How soon can we leave town and disappear forever?" Mazie whimpered as she settled into the car.

"But sweetie, that was an amazing feat. I've been telling you for years you've been hiding your light under a bushel of clothes. Many people will look on this as a revelation! An epiphany, even," he snorted, trying to maintain some semblance of sympathy but feeling hard pressed.

"Epiphany, my fanny!" snarled Mazie.

"Exactly," said Hugh, in one great burst of laughter.

"You wouldn't know an epiphany if it bit you on the butt," said Mazie. She was reluctantly grasping the humour of the situation.

"You wait 'til we get home sweetheart. We'll look it up in the dictionary. I'll bet you your red garters! Epiphany was rampant in that hall tonight."

After they had checked Mazie out for bruises and abrasions, changed out of their party duds and poured a glass of wine for each of them, Hugh brought out the dictionary.

"So, the bet is that if you could call that fiasco an epiphany, you get my garter belt, right?" Mazie challenged. "What are you going to do with it?"

"I'm going to hang it over the rear view mirror of my pick-up truck and display it proudly!" said Hugh.

"That's going to present some difficulty from several continents away," replied Mazie, squinting at him.

"Three loops around the downtown core will be all that's required for a decent impact."

Hugh MacKenzie knew exactly what his wife needed to regain her equilibrium. A good laugh was usually the ticket. "Now are you ready for the word on 'epiphany'?" he questioned.

"Hold on, hold on. What do I get if you strike out and my awkward attempt to moon an entire convention of delegates is simply that? Not the other?"

"Well, darlin', you get to be my slave for the rest of the weekend in gratitude for the timely rescue I handled so gallantly."

"Like that's fair! And what if I have to spend the weekend in bed to recuperate?"

"I'm counting on joining you, Maze. I'm a free man. Charlie Burns can sort things out for himself and I'm sure he'll do the company proud. Now, enough stalling, let's settle this argument, okay?"

Hugh began to flip through the dictionary, holding it at different lengths from his face and tilting it at various angles toward the light. Mazie rolled her eyes, reached for her glasses and held them out to him. He took them, mumbling about the small print, and hung them on his nose. "Here we go," he said, " 'epimere,' 'epinasty,' 'epipelagic' and Yes! Epiphany! Are you ready?"

"If you're waiting for a drum roll, forget it. Just give me the definition!"

"Oh this is good, Maze. The first definition is exactly what I thought the first time I laid eyes on you. Wanna hear it?"

"Like I have a choice," groaned Mazie. "Can we get on with this?"

"It says, 'epiphany . . . appearance or manifestation of a divine being.'" He looked up at her with a grin from ear to ear. "That was you Maze! I felt like I had been hit by a bolt of lightning the first time I saw you. Remember? I was pole-axed, tongue-tied!"

"As opposed to tonight. What else is there? That definition does not describe the situation we found ourselves in this evening. And you know as well as I do that 'epiphany' has a spiritual connotation. Keep going."

"Well, I think we're getting closer. But I don't see the word 'spiritual' mentioned even once. How about . . . 'a sudden manifestation or perception of the essential nature or meaning of something'? You have to admit it all happened suddenly. I mean one minute you are walking sedately along beside me and the next minute you're arse over tea kettle! I don't think there was too much variance in the perception of 'the essential nature' of your lovely knickers, do you? Nor the body inside them."

Hugh couldn't remember a time when he had enjoyed that seething look of frustration on his wife's face more than he was doing that night. "Well," he said, wisely, "if that doesn't do it for you, how's this? 'Epiphany . . . an intuitive grasp of reality through something (as an event) usually simple and striking.' You see Maze, as I've been telling you for years, those subdued colours you wear are not really 'you.' And the 'event' tonight, simple and striking as it was, provided an intuitive grasp of reality, regarding your true colours, to everyone else in the hall. I think you might be right up there with Saint Bernadette and Our Lady of Lourdes when 'epiphany' is discussed in this town from now on."

"Hugh MacKenzie, you are so full of it!" Mazie reached out to take a swipe at him and her face crumpled in pain.

"Come on, sweetheart. Let's go get you some ibuprofen and ice for your back."

"That sounds good."

"You can start your servitude when you're feeling better."

"You never give up, do you?"

"Never. You'd be on me like a wolf. I saw it all in an epiphany once."

"Did you ever consider a life in the Church?" asked Mazie dryly.

"Not a chance! Why do you ask?"

"You might be interested in exploring the possibilities of an eternity in hell," said Mazie, glaring at him.

Hugh laughed. "Nah, as long as I have you, Maze, life is a little slice of heaven. I'm content. But I think we should go shopping when you're up to it. If you ever get the itch to display your wares so openly again I think you should consider the impact that black could have for your encore performance."

"Enough!" said Mazie. "Epiphanies do not do repeat engagements. Everybody will have to milk this one to the full extent. Which I am sure they will do. And I don't need an epiphany to convince me of that."

Reedy Woman

By Anita L. Trapler

Reedy woman bent and stooped
your face so long and sad.
Paper thin creases circle your eyes
while gentle breezes caress the plowed
furrows of your face.
A testimony to the life you've had.
You sweep your hands through your glittering hair.
Silver strands fly up to the tips of branches of an old
cherry tree; its leaves are droopy in the afternoon sun.
So while you stand in this dusty street,
birds flit and flee from the shimmery tinsel in
that old cherry tree.
Do you long to fly away in a heartbeat?
Are you alone? To whom shall you go?
What will brighten the shadows of your day?

Then, a neighbour clasps your hands
and kisses your brow.
Reedy woman you stand tall.
A dazzling smile reveals the beauty of your face.
Yet is it only the artist who sees the beauty of your
face and can reveal your grace?
Reedy woman, I know your real name.
But I shan't tell.

Hey, Mom, remember when?

By Jody Chadderton

Remember when you looked at me for the first time, red-faced and squawking, plump and bald like a little old man? Remember counting my twenty little digits before pronouncing me absolutely perfect and taking me in your arms?

Remember the name you gave me, Mom, the special little nickname that was mine alone? What songs did you sing to me, Mom, when I was a baby? I haven't heard you sing for a long time. Please tell me you still sing along when a favourite song is played or when the choir sings your favourite Christmas carol.

What did you talk to me about when the two of us stayed up late together or when I woke you up in the middle of the night and we shared rare moments alone? When I made little baby-talk noises, did you answer with gibberish, or did you answer life's big questions for me? Did you tell me about current events, politics, fashion, economics or did we discuss laundry, shopping lists and new recipes? Did you worry about the world your daughters would grow up in? Did you wonder what opportunities we would have?

1957. Lester Pearson was awarded the Nobel Peace Prize, the Milwaukee Braves beat the Yankees in the World Series, postage stamps were three cents, the Russians launched Sputnik I, Humphrey Bogart died and Elvis was king. You always let me know how much you believed in me. I could do anything. I could be anything. I wonder if you thought I would grow up to be a famous celebrity, a politician, an astronaut.

Do you remember that day when your little bald-headed baby got up and ran? I think you said I was only 7 or 8 months old. If I had been born first, we would know for sure. There's always a baby book for the first-born, a record of first words, first steps, first teeth. For the second baby, there may or may not be a book, but the entries are never consistent and meticulous. By the time you have a third child, you might as well not even enter the baby's name in the book — better to just give it away still in the original box to the next mom to have a first-born child.

Okay, so my baby book has too many blank pages, testament to the busy life of my mother. Still, I have precious souvenirs of my baby days: silver mug, silver baby spoon with the curved handle for pudgy fingers to grasp, a heart-shaped locket with my christening date, a bronzed shoe which once held a very small, very quick foot. A foot made for running and leaping and tripping down the basement stairs.

Oh, I was such a clever baby to figure out the latch on the baby gate, open the gate, take the shortest route to the basement floor. What was so great about the basement?

Letters from Osoyoos

By Maureen Olson

1878

Dearest MaMa,

When this letter reaches you, we will be settled in our temporary house. I do not wish to cause you extra worry but the Custom House, our first home, burned down because of a chimney fire. We are all well and coping even though it was a terrible setback. Our quick recovery can be attributed to the kindness of the community. We moved into the Court House for the present. Generous neighbours provided necessities until Judge Haynes could get us what we needed. He is starting to plan the location for the replacement Customs House and our home. I can not give you more details now. The pack train is leaving in the morning so I'll just add news about the children. . .

1879

Dearest MaMa,

This year I can tell you more about our future home. It will be located on the shore of Osoyoos Lake, just south of the trail down the very steep mountain to the east and on the edge of a sandy beach. It will be set back from the shore, we're relieved to know, to allow for high water during spring run-off. There is a flat area around the site for the livery barn and other out-buildings. This past winter, the large stones for the foundation were brought down the mountain on stone boats pulled by teams of horses. We thanked God when they arrived safely with no injuries to beasts or man. The logs for the primary floor support are now secured to the rocks.

In December I had a midwife come for my lying-in which was safe and successful. You have another grandson, William Edgar, to note in the family bible. The weather was so bad that the midwife did not go back home until March. We enjoyed her help. As for our family . . .

1880

Dearest MaMa,
We had great excitement this spring. The lumber for the new house arrived. A list of needed lumber had been delivered to the mill at Okanagan Landing in the fall. It is the nearest, just 120 miles north on Okanagan Lake. We heard in April that the order was ready but delivery was delayed until run-off was finished so it could be safely rafted down the lake. I could not visualize what it would look like as I have not traveled to that distant area.

One day in May there was excitement outside. Some of the cowboys rode into the yard shouting, "It's coming! It's coming! Come with the wagon so you'll be able to see the raft coming through the narrows."
We all rushed out to the wagon which was ready to go. I looked forward to having the farm manager explain these events to me. He said:

The lumber was floated in the lake, bundled together with ropes to make a raft. A mast and sails were raised to push the floating lumber steadily down the lake, the 50 miles to Penticton. One day a strong wind from the south forced the beaching of the lumber until it died down. Yes, we did tie up during darkness. In one area, there was a waterfall so the lumber had to be untied, carried board by board past the falls, then re-stacked and tied so it could be floated down the river to the next lake, then down the next river into two other small lakes before coming to the north end of Osoyoos Lake.

As the lumber left the north end of Okanagan Lake, it sailed past the village of Kelowna, attracting many people to the shore to see it. Boats were not able to cross in front of the large mass of lumber so some followed behind for several miles. There were four other communities where the residents came out in force to see such a large lumber raft and to wonder where it was going. In fact I heard bets were taken on the duration of this trip.

As soon as the raft was through the narrows I hurried the team and wagon home so I could prepare a celebration for the crew who had worked so hard to bring our lumber here. Now we wait for construction to begin.

As for news of the children . . .

1881

Dearest MaMa,
We have a house! It has 10 rooms, an impressive sun-dried clay brick fireplace at each end of the main room and a veranda, 10 feet wide on all sides. Two of the rooms on the main floor are the Custom House, the remainder of the building is our home. The second floor has two large rooms, one for the boys and one for the girls, and two other bedrooms. It is such a luxury to have a bedroom for myself. Now when families visit us, they are able to stay overnight.

The outside second kitchen has already been used this summer to allow the preserving of fruits and vegetables without getting the house too hot. We are waiting for windows to come by pack horse from Hope. I'm keeping my fingers crossed the horses will be sure-footed as they traverse the mountain trails. This trip usually takes eight to ten days, depending on the weather.

The outside of the house was sheeted with clapboards. Inside, cheesecloth was tacked to cover the clapboards. Next year, we will glue the wallpapers I have selected and ordered from Vancouver, on this cheesecloth. We do not know when it will arrive.

We had so much ice on the lake this winter we built an ice house. We put blocks of ice in it with sawdust around them. It worked well, just like the one you have at home. Everyone was amazed when we served jellied fruit at a dinner in July.

And now the news of our growing children . . .

Details obtained from the Okanagan Historical Society.

Miss Eames

By Allene Halliday

Whenever I bake, whether it be cookies, breads or cakes, I remember my long ago high school junior year's Home Economics class. Actually, not the class so much as the instructor, Miss Eames.

Baking wasn't something I was anxious to learn at age sixteen. I was an aspiring performer; I had to be careful about my diet. Singing and dancing were my principal interests with boys coming in a distant third. Cookies, breads and cakes had no place on that list. Nonetheless, Home Economics was a requirement. Sewing with Mrs. McNary had been last semester's class. Baking with Miss Eames was this semester's. Reluctantly, I went into her room and took a seat next to the sinks.

Making an unpleasant situation worse, Miss Eames was not my favorite teacher. She wasn't fun and imaginative like Mr. Kramer, my algebra instructor. Nor was she petite and dramatic like Miss Farnham, who taught French and English.

Instead, Miss Eames was rigid and severe. Her hair was steely gray, wiry and tightly curled close to her head. Her two front teeth protruded and there was a pronounced gap between them. She wore unbecoming dresses in insipid blue, gray or green shades. They all appeared to be tailored in the same unflattering style: long sleeves, tiny collars, buttons down the bodice front from neck to waist, straight skirts reaching to midcalf and narrow belts. Every dress accentuated her thin, straight figure and big bones. In addition, she towered over everyone in the class. Although she smiled often, it was not in a warm, friendly way. Her smiles made us cringe.

None of us liked her.

"You must measure carefully. DO NOT WASTE FOOD," she admonished us.

Cupfuls of flour had to be measured precisely, even with the rim. Excess flour was carefully scraped off the top, with the back of a knife, onto a sheet of wax paper. That excess went back into the flour bin.

"Don't spill anything on the floor. That's wasteful," she'd sharply remind us as she paced between our work stations.

We were cautioned just as carefully about the measurement of spoonfuls of spices and shortening. Miss Eames was consistent — and adamant.

She didn't trust us with the liquids. Those she measured beforehand and set out, ready to use, in glass jars beside the mixing bowls and wooden spoons on the work tables.

Mom never had much time to bake because she worked full time at J. C. Penney's. This was especially the case at Christmastime when she had to work extra hours at the store. That winter I was to handle the baking chores. I was to put into practice what I was learning at school. (My older sister had already opted to do the ironing while my younger sister only had to dry the dishes.) Mom handed me the big, blue, almost new all purpose cookbook.

"Your Aunt Mil gave me this a few years ago. I've barely looked at it. See if you can find a recipe for a nice coffeecake to start off with. It's one of the easiest desserts to make."

It's a wonder I continued with my designated responsibility. My first coffeecake was a disaster! It came out of the oven over-baked with huge craters all across the surface where the brown sugar topping had eaten its way through to the bottom. Too much butter.

I did not tell Miss Eames about that coffeecake.

As to why Miss Eames insisted we be so careful: I've come to the conclusion that it had to do with her experiences during the Depression. I do not know her personal history, but I suspect she suffered during that prolonged period of abject poverty that affected so much of the world. Apparently, the lesson she learned so well and which she strove to teach us was: one must be careful or go hungry.

Following the Depression, during the Second World War, our country's population was encouraged not to waste food because people in Europe and Asia were starving.

Miss Eames had more than a decade and a half to learn her stringent ways.

When I told Mom about how precise the measurements had to be, she remarked, "Oh, and I always use less than the recipe calls for." Mom went through the Depression, too.

Once our teacher carried her demands for precision way too far; we spent a whole period, FIFTY MINUTES, learning to make toast (not too light and not too dark) and how to butter it properly (spread it evenly to the very edges, but not over the edges). Between yawns and giggles, it was all we could do to get through that class. Afterwards, in the schoolyard, we revelled in criticizing her unmercifully (behind her back and out of earshot, of course).

A short time later, the poor lady was taken ill with the flu. For an entire week we teenagers blissfully enjoyed the substitute instructor's class. She was cheerful, laughed often and was s-o-o-o easy-going about our cooking efforts. There was no peering over our shoulders as we worked, no chastising if our measurements weren't exact, and, often, she'd finish the cleanup duties if we ran out of time. That never would have happened with Miss Eames.

Then, the following week, in the school office, where I worked as part of my secretarial training, I read the teachers' bulletin that Miss Eames had died of pneumonia. Information about the time and place of her funeral completed the notice. I was horrified remembering how happy I'd been when she was out sick.

But I had not wanted her to die. None of us had wanted that.

She might come back to haunt us.

From this distance of more than half a century, I remember her fondly. Really, I do! Baking has given me so much pleasure. I enjoy the entire process: clearing off the counter, setting out the mixing bowl, measuring cup and spoons and preparing the pans. Of course, the actual mixing is my favorite part. It is a sort of magic, an alchemy of sorts, the way diverse ingredients combine to create an often delectable treat. Am I as careful as Miss Eames instructed me to be? I try to be, but I don't always follow recipes exactly. Occasionally, the results are as bad as my first coffeecake and I guiltily remember her admonition, "Don't waste food!"

If she ever does come back to haunt me, I have this message for her: "This is a bit late, but thank you, Miss Eames. You did your best always to teach your recalcitrant students valuable lessons. The world might be in better shape today had there been a few more teachers like you."

I can just hear her reply, "It is too bad I did not teach you how to measure liquids properly. Do be more careful, Allene!"

The Best Medicine

By Maureen Kresfelder

I was euphoric. I would be home at least 5 days with the chicken pox. My brother, Jim, would be away at school. I would have my mother all to myself. At last, I would have her full attention.

In 1949, my mother, a war widow, had little time to spend with her 8 year old daughter and 9 year old son. She was too busy chopping wood for the stove, feeding coal to the furnace, cleaning house, cooking, doing yard work or sewing and mending for her family and her home business.

But my euphoria was short-lived. The moment my brother left for school my mother ordered me back to bed. I was sick, she said, and needed rest. She pulled down the blinds, closed the lined curtains and stuck a thermometer in my mouth.

"You have to lie in the dark. Light aggravates the eyes and causes headaches when you've got chicken pox," she informed me. "I'll get you some calamine lotion." My pox was at the red pimply stage and very itchy. "In the meantime, don't scratch."

Mother never minced words nor mollycoddled her children. She came back and checked my temperature. "You have a slight fever — nothing to worry about though. Unfortunately, we've run out of calamine — I'll have to buy some more. But first drink this - this will help you get better." She handed me a glass of cod liver oil and orange juice. "But Mother," I protested, "I don't feel that bad. Honest." My protestations and genuine tears were to no avail. Cod liver oil and orange juice was her remedy for everything from a broken thumb nail to life threatening illnesses. She watched me drink it, ignoring the exaggerated gagging sounds I made, till every last oily, fishy drop had slithered its way into my stomach.

Being at home was not going the way I planned. I had fantasized that my mother would read me a story like she did on the odd "free" weekend. (Normally, she used every evening to sew for customers). Then I would chat with her about the story or how Jackie and his little brother, Frankie, were always teasing me about my unruly red hair and long spindly legs. And she would give me sensible advice about how to deal with the teasing. I never told her that I ignored her advice and simply threatened kids who bugged me with my older brother. He was nine and loved to fight. He did come in handy from time to time.

She told me she would ask Mrs. Baillie from next door to baby sit while she went to the drugstore to get some calamine lotion. Thankfully, Mrs. Baillie was not home. She was crotchety and had a mustache and beady eyes. Her husband, Mother said, worked a lot of overtime. And, I had observed, stared hypnotically at my mother's chest.

Mother made me swear that I wouldn't leave the house or the bed. In case of emergency I was to go across the street to get Mrs. Best, a retired British nurse, who spoke with an I'm-better-than-you accent. She agreed only to "watch the house" from her living room while Mother ran her errand. "Apparently you're contagious," my mother said. "Even I know that your contagious phase has passed. Why can't she at least be honest and say she doesn't like kids?"

The minute my mother closed the door I got out of bed. I felt a twinge of guilt about breaking my promise to stay in bed. But I rationalized I had earned hundreds of Brownie points with God by taking all that cod liver oil. I played with my dolls briefly and then my brother's Meccano set. I knew it would bug him when he found out and I would be sure to tell him.

I soon got bored with my toys and my brother's. Besides, I was scratching like mad. And I felt feverish, irritable and very sorry for myself. I needed a more compelling distraction.

Something to make me forget about my itching and the revolting aftertaste of the cod liver oil that was still oozing its way through my beleaguered intestines. As I glanced idly around the room I spied my roller skate key hanging on a hook by my closet. Did I dare?

I knew that my mother, on foot, would be at least an hour. It was over 6 blocks to the drugstore. And then she usually checked out the specials and gossiped a bit with the druggist. I could skate for at least 15 minutes and still have time to get back in bed and compose myself. I was excited by my daring. I quickly put my clothes overtop my pajamas. That would save time. And I tidied up my toys. I prided myself on thinking ahead like Nancy Drew.

But I couldn't leave by the front door. Mrs. Best was sure to be watching, lurking in the shadows of her living room. I'd have to go out the back lane.

On the back steps I strapped on my skates and tightened them with my key. I opened the back gate and skated gingerly on the rough tarmac of the lane. I went up the lane for three blocks and then onto the sidewalk. Mrs. Best would surely never think to look three blocks up the street.

I skated up and down the sidewalk with ever increasing speed, the fresh spring breeze cooling my fevered brow. Skating was the best medicine for chicken pox. I forgot about my itchy skin, I forgot about the cod liver oil, I forgot about being sentenced to bed. When I skated I went places I never imagined I'd go when bound to the earth by my feet. I crossed wild oceans with Jonathan and the Pirates, galloped after bandits with Roy Rogers and Dale Evans, flew with Amelia Earhart to exotic lands.

Every time I got to the crest of our hill I checked to see if Mother were coming. I had three good skates up the street and down before I saw her homemade navy coat and hat far in the distance. I quickly got off the street, removed my skates and ran down the lane and into the house. I disrobed, hastily hung up my street clothes, turned off the light and got into bed. I had barely pulled up the covers when I heard the front door open. Mother, laden with purchases, poked her head into the bedroom and asked, "How are you feeling, little one?"

"Not too bad, Mom," I said in a sickly voice. "Just a bit itchy. Could you read me a story? I think I'd feel much better then."

She said she'd be right with me once she had put the perishables in the ice box. She came into the darkened bedroom and switched on a lamp.

"Oh my goodness, child, you look so flushed." She felt my forehead and gasped. "You're burning up, you're sweating. I'm going to get Mrs. Best."

"Mom I'm fine," I said hastily and more spiritedly. "Honestly. I don't feel all that sick." I sat up in bed and smiled brightly, moving my head from side to side in a playful manner.

"Now, don't be silly," she said sternly. "You lie down and be still. Mrs. Best will know what to do." I groaned which she mistook for pain. "You poor thing," she said. She headed for the door.

"Wait," I called. I scrambled out of bed and ran after her praying that Mary, mother of Jesus, would miraculously come to my aid. I reckoned it took no less than Jesus' mother to intercede on my behalf. I was convinced that Mary had a special influence with mothers. She had rescued me on more than one occasion when I'd been disobedient. I just hoped she wasn't fed up with me yet.

"Mom," I said grabbing her arm, "wait, please. I have something to tell you." I spoke fast and furiously so I wouldn't lose my nerve. "I was playing outside, roller skating actually, when you were gone. That's why I'm so hot and sweaty. You don't need to get Mrs. Best. Honest. I'm okay. I really am. Really."

Mother looked at me astonished, momentarily speechless. Then she put her hands on her hips, the stance she took when Jim and I had committed major sins. "Maureen Gaye Carney," she said angrily, "are you telling me that when I went to the store you disobeyed me, got out of your sick bed and roller-skated?" I nodded contritely and hung my head.

"Look at me when I talk to you, young lady."

I raised my head, my face and throat aflame with pox, my curly red hair wild and wind blown, my eyes brimming with tears of remorse. I stood slumped, my pjs hanging limply and damply on my bony frame. As I looked at her and she looked at me her lips began to twitch. She covered her mouth with her hands laughing silently, then coughing and choking as she tried to suppress the laughter that would not stop. Soon, her laughter was pealing out like unruly church bells. She was laughing so hard that she had to sit down, literally overcome by the force of her mirth. I had never heard her laugh like this, never seen her lose control of her emotions. Not knowing what to do, I stood there wide-eyed, anxiously waiting to see what would happen next. One thing was certain, I had her full attention.

After her laughter subsided, she looked at me and held out her arms. She hugged me, then lifted me onto the bed with her. She said, "I'm so glad you're feeling okay – well, more than okay. And that you told me the truth, as hard as that was."

As if embarrassed by this outburst of sentiment, she added quickly and severely, "That doesn't mean I approve of what you did, mind you. Now get into bed and I'll put the calamine lotion on you." And then winking at me, she added more softly, "If you think you're up to it, I'll read you a story. Would you like that?"

When Jim came home from school I called out to him, "Hey Jim, com'ere a minute." Jim reluctantly sauntered into my sick room after Mother said I was not contagious. But he stopped in the middle of the room, just in case.

"Don't want any girl germs. Whaddya want?"

I smiled sweetly. "Guess what? Mother just read me two of our favourite stories, you know, about Jonathan and the pirates and that new cowboy one and you'd better check your Meccano set. Mother said I could play with it. Not sure if I put everything back the way you had it. How was school?"

A Level of Control

By Sue Whittaker

Despite her best efforts, Marianne's evening was not going well. Kenneth, as a date, was losing his appeal rapidly. She had dragged him through the previous dance. Drowning kittens would have been more fun.

By this time in the evening she might have been out to a car twice for the euphemistic "smoke." Each time she would have established the level of control necessary to maintain the fine line between growing male eagerness and the seemliness expected at a high school dance.

Trying once more, Marianne tugged Kenneth up from his chair. For him to have resisted further would have caused too great a scene. But it soon became clear to her that no amount of cuddling or snuggling in the low light improved his focus. Marianne began to feel that perhaps his attention strayed elsewhere. This was not a concern she had faced previously in her dating experience. She was the one who called it quits. Never had she been dumped!

"And doesn't this just top it all," she muttered as she returned from the washroom in time to see Kenneth leaving the building. She sensed a furtive haste in his quiet exit, his fingers had slowed the heavy door, bringing it to a soft, hissing rest.

Taking equal care, Marianne followed, not so much to retrieve a reluctant date as to pursue an unfolding mystery.

The night pungency of the pine woods that half encircled the school grounds lent an edge to her escalating curiosity. Although only seconds behind her quarry, he was not to be seen in any of the open areas. She cast a glance toward the trees and some movement, or glint of light, drew her attention to the left; two figures, both male, both tall and dark, melting into the backdrop of evergreens.

Any lingering hope of rescuing the evening left Marianne's mind. She was on the scent of something much more interesting riding on the late spring breeze.

No deep male laughter, no trail of cigarette smoke, no jostling banter guided her. But they were in there, surely hiding something. But what?

Inching forward in the dark, edging from tree to tree, she sensed their presence. Rough breathing, the rustle of clothing, gasps of intense emotional struggle — she recognized the signs.

Then awareness slammed through her, throwing her somehow off balance. She clasped a tree, resting her face against the rugged bark, silently pleading, God, help me or take me right now! This was more than she was prepared to deal with on her own. One of the muffled voices was sounding more and more like Mr. Jenks, the principal.

"Easy now, There's a good lad." His signature phrase. No doubt at all now whom Kenneth had met with in the dark.

Marianne dreaded the risk of exposure. Her sense of adventure deserted her. She trembled and clung to the pine tree, immobilized with fear and trapped. Trapped by the possibility that retreat would signal her presence, leading to humiliation, the stigma of a Peeping Tom.

This situation was more than she had bargained for. Who would even believe her if she were to speak of it? Did she have a responsibility to expose such a relationship? Was Kenneth there willingly? Had he been coerced? Was he enjoying it? Did he need help?

Doing nothing proved to be exceptionally wise. Eventually an audible struggle for restraint was achieved by the hapless couple. "Come now, lad. Pull yourself together. We must go back in."

"What's happening? What's gonna happen?" sobbed Kenneth. Marianne briefly glimpsed a strong arm circle Kenneth's shoulder, calming him. Tension dissipated and she followed the sound of their footsteps moving off.

Grateful to have maintained cover, and gradually released from fear, Marianne began to consider her options.

Kenneth was of course, a lost cause.

Mr. Jenks though, might become . . . manageable. If she had the courage. Subtle revelation, followed by the assurance of her discretion, might prove useful to her whole graduating class. But how to go forward?

After the lunch break on Monday, Marianne entered the school snuggled under the broad shoulder of her friend, Butch, their arms around each others' waists. As expected, they were cut from the herd and directed to Mr. Jenks' office. Snuggling did not fall within the realm of acceptable behaviour at their high school.

"What are you two trying to prove here?" the principal snarled. "You know that type of behaviour is forbidden in the halls. The Grade Twelve class is expected to set an example for the rest of the school."

Butch glared at Mr. Jenks in his usual insolent manner. She had chosen him for his amazing ability to resist intimidation. Marianne took a big breathe and raised her eyes innocently. "Are you suggesting we sneak out to the woods then?"

She refused to look away as Mr. Jenks' eyes flickered in shocked disbelief and a tide of red anger swept up his neck, quickly colouring his whole head. Although Marianne's heart was pounding and she held her hands behind her back to hide the trembling, she refused to back down or respond to his threats.

"Butch, you can leave," Mr. Jenks said.

"I think I'll stay," Butch said, crossing his arms over his chest and taking a firm stance.

Mr. Jenks turned his attention to Marianne. "You can't come in here and threaten me. I could have you suspended from school."

"Go ahead," dared Marianne. "I can tell everyone what I saw happening between you and Kenneth on Friday night. You have a way more to lose than I do."

"This is blackmail!" he gasped, moving towards her.

Butch stepped forward and Mr. Jenks backed off.

Eventually, not withstanding an impressive display of rage and bluster, an agreement was adopted between the two of them. It was tacitly agreed that it would be the best thing all around for her to keep his little secret. But that secret would become a valuable asset, a bargaining chip for Marianne on behalf of her graduating class.

An overbearing administrative dictum, regulating the lengths of mini skirts and the height of beehive hairdos, was toned down through her negotiation.

The senior boys' basketball team was, surprisingly, given a second chance after a major infraction involving alcohol and girls on a road trip; all restrictions were lifted after a written apology was accepted by Mr. Jenks.

Marianne's last act of defiance was in response to widespread grumblings about the band that had been hired for the graduation dance — the same band that had performed for at least a decade. She volunteered to act as emissary to the principal. So eventually, the standing engagement of "The Starlight Serenaders," was overlooked in favour of "Big Daddy," a rock band that introduced the old gymnasium to rattling windows and vibrating floorboards.

The crunch of final exams relieved the pressure on Marianne as spokesperson for her class. The last month of school would impose different priorities on her classmates — pursuing scholarships, bursaries, university registration, summer jobs and making career choices. The weekend bush parties, spontaneous events involving nothing more challenging than a bonfire and beer, took place without her help.

Her top priority was to get out of town. She had walked the fine line between leadership and manipulation, teetered between headiness and fear, long enough. A nice little secretarial course, a job in an office, a boss she could impress with her management skills . . . .

"Work with your strengths," her counselors told her.

She would.

My Favourite Shirt

By Jody Chadderton

I almost forgot to change my shirt before I went out. I was wearing my favourite shirt, well-worn and comfy, not a shirt to wear to a meeting. The shirt is a grey hooded pullover like what we used to call a kangaroo jacket or roo for short, but these days it's called a hoodie. Unlike the classic roo or hoodie, my shirt has no pocket or kangaroo pouch in front, and for some reason, it is also missing the casing and drawstring around the hood. It has the standard ribbed cuffs though and the ribbed waistband, both frayed to ragged edges. The sleeves are not quite long enough to accommodate my arms, but by pushing them up to three-quarter length, I am able to partially hide the holes in the left elbow. The holes have been there for a long time, the result of a skidding crash on the pavement. I remember being airborne for what seemed like several seconds after Trouble, the beagle pup, crossed in front of me while we were running. I also remember Trouble standing over me as I cursed and tried to pick myself up. Trouble wagging his tail and dancing around ready to resume our jog when I gingerly got to my feet. I glanced around furtively to see if there were witnesses to my acrobatics; then looked down at my skinned knees both dripping blood now and dotted with grit. My right hand was also grazed, but my left elbow sustained less injury, the brunt having been borne by the fleecy fabric of my favourite shirt. I felt like a kid again, I remember thinking, but not in a good way.

I smile now as I pull the sweatshirt over my head, remembering how silly those scabby knees had looked when I was thirty-something. And I shake off the thought that thirty-something was a long time ago.

Ripe Old Age

By Sue Whittaker

She twists in front of the mirror
viewing her right hip, her left hip,
front and back.
The roundness, the rumpy-ness,
astounds her once again.

No amount of sacrifice, self-denial or deprivation
has subdued her tendency
toward the voluptuous.
She can be genetically traced, she groans,
to a Bartlett, an Anjou or a roly-poly little Bosc.
Oh well, perhaps she will live to a ripe old age.

An Unforgettable Weekend

By Allene Halliday

In 1994, I took my mom to Orcas Island, in the San Juans north of Seattle, to spend the weekend before Christmas at Rosario Resort. She was ninety-three years old and quite fragile. When a winter's storm blew in, the morning we were to set out on this trip, I questioned the wisdom of our going.

But Mom was excited and looking forward to it, so I couldn't bring myself to cancel now. I loaded her wheelchair into the back of the car and we began our adventure.

The wheelchair had not been easy for her to accept. She'd always stubbornly insisted on maintaining her independence. Just a few years prior to this, when Mom first began to have difficulty walking, her brother gave her a cane that he had lovingly carved out of a beautiful piece of manzanita (one of Mom's favorite trees). She unceremoniously refused his gift by threatening to hit him over the head with it. A cane (even this marvelous piece of workmanship created by her favorite brother) represented for her that dreaded consequence of old age: infirmity!

Yet, she now accepted the wheelchair without protest or complaint. It was a huge, but quietly made, concession to reality on her part.

Mom was not alarmed by the bumpy ride to Orcas on the small but sturdy old ferry as we crossed the rough waters. She had lived for years within view of the ferry landing in Anacortes on Fidalgo Island. While still independent, she'd made innumerable trips to various islands aboard these colorful transports in all kinds of weather. She usually knew members of the crew, and would visit with them as well as with the other passengers.

People brought out Mom's vivacious personality.

However, this trip it was too dangerous for her to go out to the passenger cabin. We had to stay in the car. Since we were parked at the front of the ferry, there was no lack of entertainment. We experienced the thrill of watching waves repeatedly crashing over the bow of the tiny craft and splashing against our windshield.

As we drove from the landing to the resort, I noticed there were several recently uprooted trees near the road. This storm was unquestionably a severe one! My nervousness about this outing grew. But it was too late to turn back.

The first evening there was a program about the history of the resort and the early twentieth century mansion at the center. Originally this tourist spot had been the home of Seattle business tycoon, Robert Moran. Mom was fascinated by the history of the Northwest and was looking forward to this presentation. Unfortunately, we discovered that it would take place on the mezzanine, which was reached by an impressive, long staircase. There was no elevator! Mother was tiny; she measured less than five feet tall and weighed a mere ninety pounds. Still, I couldn't carry her up those stairs — with or without the wheelchair.

I wheeled Mom to one side at the base of the stairs in order for her to be close enough, perhaps, to hear the program above. Then I went up to catch a glimpse of the lecture hall so I could describe it to her.

As I stood at the entrance to the room, the narrator stopped midsentence to invite me in to take a seat. "I'm sorry," I explained. "I need to go back downstairs to be with my mom. She can't climb up the stairs."

Immediately, three gentlemen in the audience jumped up and rushed down to her. They lifted Mom up, chair and all, as I stood by helplessly wringing my hands. She was carried, unresisting but surprised, quickly up the stairs.

When the program ended, these gentlemen whisked her safely back down. It would be difficult to say whether it was their gallantry or the presentation that was the highlight of the evening for Mom.

During dinner in the formal dining area overlooking the harbor, we enjoyed musical entertainment provided by the talented pianist, who had earlier been the program narrator. He was playing seasonal music on the elegant grand piano that dominates the center of this room.

Mom decided to make a request of him. I helped her limp over to the pianist, who recognized us, smiled, and graciously listened to her. "I'd like for my daughter to sing *White Christmas* while you accompany her."

I was surprised, but was willing to do it.

Without hesitation he asked what key I would like and the next moment I was on. It was as though we had spent hours rehearsing the number. He didn't miss a beat and I didn't miss a word. Mom was in heaven!

Next evening we went into the lounge to sit by the huge, dark wooden fireplace as we listened to a combo of three musicians. This warm, inviting room reminded us of the paneled living room and brick fireplace in our former home in Anacortes. I ordered wine and we began reminiscing about past Christmases. Mom enjoyed a glass of good wine whenever the occasion merited one. This occasion certainly did!

It was after midnight when we got up to return to our room. Mom would have liked to stay longer in the lounge, but the musicians were packing up to leave and I was worn out.

Whenever I hear Irving Berlin's lovely Christmas song that my mom requested at Rosario, I relive that incomparable weekend. It was our last trip together. What a happy, memorable time we had — storm and all!

Suspended Surprise

By Maureen Olson

Can I create excitement
when presenting the ring to my love?

Blindfold her? A scavenger hunt?
Kneel to declare my pledge?
No!

Ah! A bang from a burst balloon.
My ring will drift down
to eye level.

Small balloon with ring attached,
threaded into a larger one;
both inflated.

Nerve-wracking walk,
I clutch the balloon
from store, to car, to house.

She struggles to puncture the balloon
as I hold it within her reach.
After one, two, three attempts,
our laughter becomes hysterical.

I steady her hand.
One thrust with the pin
then the Big Bang!

Floating in front of her eyes . . .
the ring.
She screams!

Signs of Improvement

By Sue Whittaker

"Dad, Mom wants to know if you need anything from town before she starts home."

"Tell the hag to get back here 'toot sweet' and make me my dinner!"

"No, Mom, he says he's fine. Bye." Kathy hung up the phone, looked at her dad and shook her head.

"What?" he asked, laughing.

"You better get those potatoes peeled, don't you think? And you haven't mowed the grass yet or picked the beans."

"Yeh, yeh, yeh, I'm on my way," he said, setting aside his glass and hauling himself up out of the chair. "That woman doesn't know how lucky she is that I'm still around. 'Cut the grass, pick the beans, save the country!'" He threw his hands above his head. "I run out of time every day trying to keep her happy."

Kathy sat looking out at the dreary street in front of her apartment, the remembered conversation ringing in her ears. Six months ago he had seemed like a rock, the granite shield their family was built on, not to mention the immovable object in the way of family normality for which she longed.

But in two days he was gone, the victim of a massive stroke, an irresistible force even he was no match for.

Without him, her mother was a wreck and Christmas had been a complete bust without his shocking pronouncements. She recalled him walking into the family room with a gun when she and her brother and sister were little kids.

"Dad," her brother Brian had asked, "what are you going to do with the gun?"

"I'm going to shoot Santa in the arse if he falls down the chimney again this year. I'm tired of him tracking ashes and soot around the room. If he can't make it through the front door like everybody else, he's toast!"

The wailing and pleading from Brian was exactly the reaction he had been trying for. He laughed raucously and put the gun down. He picked the kid up by his feet, swung him around the room a few times and called him "a sissy Mommy's boy."

By this time, she and her sister Janet had learned not to react to his teasing beyond an, "Oh, Daaaad." But Brian's reaction caused a huge upheaval on Christmas Eve with accusations and threats flying between their mom and dad, all mollified as the liquor came out, and Brian was finally assured there would be no shooting.

When Brian brought Charlotte and her daughter into the family, though, Charlotte had stepped right up and told him if he tried any of that crap with his grandchildren he'd live to regret it. She had their dad's number right away. And he became so attached to "the rug rats," as he called Annie and the new baby, that he tried, somewhat successfully, to tone things down. He admitted he had met his match in "the Devil Woman."

But what was it with Mom, Kathy wondered? She had hired a jeweler to make her a locket, large enough to carry around some of Dad's ashes, next to her heart.

"I'm just not ready to let him go yet," she wept.

He *was* a hard person to replace.

In Kathy's opinion, that was a good thing. The family gene pool was showing signs of improvement.

Survival
A Life Story

By Sheila Blimke

Relaxing comfortably in our deck chairs, having vacated the dining room after our evening meal, my husband Lou and I, along with our dear friend Tom, were enjoying a gentle summer breeze. Suddenly the tranquility was shattered by sounds of squabbling emitting from the house next door, undoubtedly the result of a skirmish amongst the grandchildren.

"Stop fighting with your sister!" chuckled Tom, a smile of remembrance flitting across his face. "Words heard often by me as a child!" he added, with a laugh. "'Think of your gran,' my mother would say. 'She had eight siblings to contend with, surely you can get along with one!'"

"My Goodness, Tom!" I exclaimed. "We never knew you had that many great-aunts and uncles! Fill us in on the family!"

With some gentle prodding from Lou and me, Tom finally settled in and told us the fascinating life story of his grandmother.

"Unfortunately I have only the slightest memory of her," Tom said. "My mother took my sister and me on an extended visit to Gran's Vancouver home when I was a small child. I faintly remember her as a tiny lady, giving me plenty of hugs. After the hugs I would invariably find a candy hidden deep in my pants' pocket. This was a huge treat, since our visit with her came during the Depression, when everything was scarce, particularly candy.

"My grandmother was born in England into a working class family, during the latter part of the 19th century, the eldest of nine children. The town they lived in was built by a group of far-sighted businessmen, intent on establishing an ironworks company. They chose, as their location, an uninhabited strip of land in northeast England on the shores of the North Sea. The town and housing were first established then came the erection of the plant. Next, the search for employees began. My great-grandfather, John Brady, who was at that time residing in an area fairly close to this chosen site, was soon to arrive with his young family."

Shifting to a more comfortable position, Tom continued with his story.

"Because the plant was located near the town, it became a common practice to send the older children over with their father's midday meal. Being the eldest, and since the route skirted open vats of molten steel, thus making the trip very hazardous, this job was allotted to Mary, my Gran. During these trips to the plant she became acquainted with James Riley, a young man recently arrived from Ireland who had also secured employment with the company. Now in her late teens, Gran fell in love with this Irishman. They married and she immediately moved to his family home in Ireland — situated on a picturesque little farm nestled in view of the beautiful Mountains of Mourn. James, however, unable to find work in Ireland, was forced to remain at his job in England.

"Mary settled into the home of her widowed father-in-law, James Riley, Sr., who had been blinded in an accident at his workplace. Also resident in the home was Mary's new sister-in-law, Mary-Ann, who soon became her best friend and confidante."

Tom paused for a sip of tea, then, collecting his thoughts, carried on.

"This became a relatively pleasant, peaceful part of Mary's life. Although her new husband could make only occasional trips back to Ireland from his employment in England, they were carefully focused on saving to establish their own home. This, however, was never to be and Mary was struck with the first of many tragedies that were to follow. Her young husband fell ill with pneumonia. Fearing the loss of his job, he attempted to work through his illness. That decision cost him his life. Mary was now left with no means of financial support for herself and children since, by then, she was the mother of two-year-old Moira, (my mother) and Sean, a new-born baby son."

Tom paused again, as though visualizing the depth of his grandmother's anguish. Finally continuing, he said, "Unable to find employment in Ireland to provide for herself and her children, Gran was forced to leave her daughter in the kind, capable hands of Mary-Ann. Taking her baby son with her she returned to England in search of work. After finding employment as a live-in maid with a well-to-do British family who resided on a small estate on the outskirts of London, it then became necessary to persuade her mother to take on the care of Sean, her newborn son. Mary then settled in to her new job.

"The home in which she found employment had a ne'er-do-well son, Sylvester Pruit, who was greatly taken with her. She had little difficulty thwarting his unwelcome advances until the next disaster struck. A disease swept through Ireland killing many of its residents, one of whom was Mary-Ann. It now became immediately essential to remove her little daughter from the blind grandfather's home. Sensing Mary's desperate situation, Sylvester lost no time in pressuring her into a hasty marriage to him and allowing her to bring her little daughter home to live with them. A decision she would sorely regret.

"From this new marriage two children were born, a son, Harry, and a daughter, Leah. Soon Mary's new spouse lost interest in the duties of parenthood and returned to his carousing lifestyle. As his debauchery increased, he now became abusive to his wife and children to such an extent that his father, a good, kind man, finally arranged, unbeknownst to his son, transportation to Canada for Gran, and her daughter Leah from the second marriage. The son, Harry, would remain with his paternal grandparents in England, growing into a fine young man, only to die prematurely from an illness, in his early twenties. Prior to leaving for Canada it became essential for Mary to again plead with her mother to take on the rearing of Moira, (my mother). This solution was finally agreed upon and both children from Mary's first marriage would be raised to adulthood in England by their maternal grandmother. Sean, her son, remained permanently in England where he would marry and raise his family.

"Her daughter, Moira, my mother, would also marry, and, with her husband and baby son, eventually immigrate to Canada.

"Following her arrival in Canada, Mary was to be employed as a maid in the home of her father-in-law's brother, who had immigrated to Canada some years earlier, becoming a successful farmer.

"Not long after settling in her new home in Canada, Mary received word that Sylvester, having exhausted his search for her in England, finally realized where she must have gone. In short order he arrived at the farm demanding her return. She refused. Lying in wait for her one evening and catching her unawares, he forced her out into the fields, thrust her down an abandoned well and left her there to perish.

"Following an intensive search, Mary was found and nursed back to health. Now, fearing for his own life, her husband fled the scene, never to be seen by her again."

Tom paused, as though overwhelmed by the words he had just spoken. Lou and I waited in silence until he could continue.

"Following this harrowing experience, Gran left the farm, fearful of the return of her husband, and found employment as a cook with the railroad. Several years later, she received word from England of the death of her husband. She then remarried, for the third time, to a Railway Engineer. Shortly after their marriage her new husband decided to leave the railway and try his hand at farming, becoming relatively successful at this new endeavor. Though they settled in a fairly isolated part of western

Canada, this new lifestyle brought Gran several years of peace and happiness. From this marriage, three daughters and a son were born and during that period her daughter from the first marriage (Moira) my mother, now a young married adult, had immigrated to Canada together with her husband and baby son. Wishing to re-establish ties with her mother, Moira and her family settled into the same community. This situation delighted Mary, but again her euphoria was cut short.

"Now, heading into the 1930's, the Depression hit with full force. Mary's husband decided to return to the railway and moved his family to Vancouver.

"Though saddened by again losing close contact with her first-born child, Mary quickly fell in love with the city, reveling in its warm climate and delighted with the beautiful beaches where she could take her family for picnics and teach her children to swim. But again the tranquility in her life was short-lived. Not long after settling in Vancouver her husband was struck and killed in the rail yards, run over by a locomotive."

Tom remained silent as though realizing we all needed time to grapple with the enormity of suffering meted out to this one person. Brushing a hand over his eyes, he finally took a deep breath and said, "In spite of all these hardships, Gran, now the sole provider for her family, raised the five children remaining in her care to adulthood and saw them settled in their careers before she died."

Reaching for his hat, as he readied himself to leave, Tom rose, flashed a faintly sardonic smile and departed with the words of an old adage:

"'What doesn't kill you — strengthens you!'"

Sleeping with Barbie

By Jody Chadderton

Barbie doll eyes watch over my sleep
one hundred forty-seven pairs
of Barbie doll eyes
in the guest bedroom:

Alphabet Soup Barbie,
Coca-Cola Barbie,
McDonald's Barbie and Kelly
(her little sister, I think.)
Movie Star Barbie and Fashion Model Barbie.
Elegant African Barbie with ebony skin
and Chinese Barbie with exotic eyes
and Barbie with an Egyptian costume,
Ukrainian Barbie and one with wooden shoes.

And Barbie with Spongebob Squarepants
and with Mickey and Goofy and Donald.
Twelve Birthstone Barbies
each in evening gowns with brilliant jewels
Garnet to Turquoise.
Teacher Barbie and Nurse Barbie
and Secretary Barbie and Hair stylist Barbie.

Barbie with skis, Barbie with skates,
Barbie with roller skates and one with a skateboard,
Barbie with scuba gear, and another with a surfboard
looking very Californian with her bronze skin
and bleached hair.
Exercise Barbie and Yoga Barbie,

Barbie doing Pilates and weight training,
Kickboxing and Karate.

Barbie being Barbie, long-legged and lean.
Eye-shadowed and lip-sticked,
with good hair days every day,
no zits or broken nails,
no canceled dates, no stay at home Saturday nights.
No P.M.S. or menstrual cramps
or fat days.
No wrinkles, no droopy boobs
just perky, smiley, beautiful.
No tears, no sweat, no runny nose,
no body fluids at all.

My friend admits to nightmares:
evil nephew takes dolls out to play.

I fear my nightmares
have deeper roots.

Bettyisms

By Allene Halliday

Betty Bryant was raised on a showboat: Bryant's Showboat.

Her grandfather Sam was the first member of the family to be an owner/captain of this unique American entertainment venue. He had traded in his medicine show — wagon, horses, medicine and bottles — to make the down payment on this floating theater, as well as the barge that moved it from town to town along the Ohio and Monangahela Rivers in the mid-west.

By the time Betty was born in 1923, the helm had been taken over by her dad Captain Billy Bryant, who had married the showboat's calliope player, Josephine.

Betty's first job was playing the baby in "Uncle Tom's Cabin" when she was a few months old. As she grew, her duties grew: singer, dancer, saxophone player, ticket taker, special effects technician, and, eventually, the star of the melodramas.

Living up to the showboat owners' motto, they provided "Family entertainment, by families, for families."

In 1943, the Bryants tied up the showboat in Cincinnati for the last time. It had been one of the last of these crafts to have provided entertainment throughout the depression and into the first years of the forties. Betty and her husband Jat, who had been hired to be her leading man, set out to work in the nightclubs that were springing up all over the United States. Ten years later, I was hired for their musical revue. We toured the United States, Europe and North Africa for years. This woman with her singular background became a major influence in my life.

When I joined her troupe, she had added choreographer, costume designer and comedienne to her list of duties and accomplishments. Always a thorough-going professional, she demanded professionalism from all of her associates.

Betty was aloof most of the time, although she laughed easily and her laughter was infectious. No one could resist responding to the hilarity whether they knew what prompted it or not. At those times her cool, dignified facade disappeared, revealing a warm, irrepressible, wonderful person unable to conceal her enjoyment, and so willing to share the fun.

During the years we performed together she taught me comedy routines, dance steps, how to make gorgeous costumes, the art of quick changes and other techniques and skills required to succeed in our profession.

Still, what I remember best are the wise words this exceptional individual imparted to me in regard to everyday living. I named this timeless advice for females, The Bettyisms!

Always assume a man is married until it is proven unquestionably that he is not.

Get rid of any clothes that do not make you feel and look your best. If you don't, it is a good bet that you WILL wear them and you WILL regret doing so.

Buy yourself at least one tailored outfit. It is worth every dollar — and then some. You will look and feel like a million dollars every time you wear it!

Practice good posture. This not only shows you and your clothes off to best advantage, it is good for your mental and physical well-being.

Practice good diction. Read poetry aloud and invest in a good book on training in proper enunciation. This not only facilitates communication, it increases your awareness of how beautiful the English language is.

Never appear in public without makeup or with your hair in curlers or pin curls. This rule applies when answering the door or taking out the garbage, as well.

Talented performers do not need to use foul language to succeed. Okay, so maybe this just applies to show people.

Then again, it should make you wonder about the merit of some current "entertainment" offerings.

When I last saw Betty in Chicago during the mid-90s, she was directing comedies in the community theater in Park Ridge. She still lived by her "isms," and "Family entertainment, by families, for families" remained her guiding principle. Her daughters have become the fourth generation of Bryants in show business. Recently, I learned that one of her grandsons plans to be the fifth.

How have I done with the "Bettyisms" over the years? Except for a few outfits I intend to weed out of the closet now that I've written this piece and a couple of poorly timed trips to the garbage can — not too badly.

Moving With Our First Home

By Maureen Olson

George and I had set our wedding date before we learned he was being assigned to set up a highway construction operation in the Prince George area. It was to be a challenging and exciting job, and a promotion.

I was immersed in wedding plans. George was planning a highway construction project taking shape 30 miles into the wilderness. You could say we were on different wave lengths and not really sharing information. Different problems, different situations.

A week before the wedding, while we were both juggling several other balls, George asked me, "Gladys, do you drive? I've never seen you behind the wheel."

I sensed something in his voice. George, who was a rock, a problem solver, a straight ahead kind of guy suddenly sounded on edge, timorous, even.

Much as I would have liked to restore his equilibrium I had to admit I was a non-driver. I had lived an urban life, content to use the bus system or occasionally, a taxi.

"Why do you ask?" I inquired.

"Well, you realize don't you, that I will be driving the truck to the site and pulling our house trailer. I expected you would follow me in the Buick."

I think my face must have registered my horror. "You want me to drive your car to follow you where?" I sputtered.

"W-e-l-l, from New Westminster, north, up the Fraser Canyon, through the Cariboo towards Prince George and then east to the campsite," George explained, haltingly. As if giving it to me in installments would make the task seem more manageable.

"George," I said, taking his hands in mine. "I'll never be able to do that. We're leaving in a week! I've never been out of the lower mainland! I've never sat behind a steering wheel! Your Buick is a block long!" The rising panic in my voice alarmed me and certainly grabbed George's attention.

Calmly and quietly he said, "I'm sure you'll be able to do it. In fact, come out and I'll give you your first lesson."

All thoughts of the wedding flew out of my mind. I followed him to the car, to sit trembling in the driver's seat. Step One. But I couldn't even reach the pedals. Nor did I know that seats were adjustable at that point.

I can't believe he thinks I can do this! I whimpered to myself, white-knuckling the steering wheel. But he seemed so serious and so assured of my abilities to grasp the fundamentals of driving, I forced myself to calm down and pay attention to his instructions.

Half an hour later, he said, with a wavering smile, "You've done well! Let's stop now and we'll start again tomorrow."

We had not moved an inch. I guessed he must have thought I needed a lot of experience with this "behind the wheel" state of mind. And in hindsight, he was right. Once you get comfortable in the driver's seat, the next steps are manageable. In small doses.

For the next three days George arrived promptly to continue the indoctrination. Gradually, I was able to start the car, pull out of the driveway, drive around the block, signal, brake, stay in my lane, and back the car into the driveway —eventually without even hitting anything —shut the car off and set the emergency brake. I would be dripping with sweat and shaking by the time each lesson was over. But George kept telling me how well I was doing and that I would be ready to follow him when the time came.

Thank goodness for Alice, my bridesmaid. Although she was of the opinion I should ditch George and start over again with some guy who had realistic expectations, she kept her peace, kept me calm and ran interference between me and my weepy mom. It was Mother's view, expressed tearfully, that she would never see me (her only child) alive again once this folly was set in motion. She had failed to make it through her first driving lesson with my dad, a trauma not forgotten by Dad either. The mother of the bride needed comforting. I couldn't do that as well. Alice coped.

Everything seemed to pass in a blur. We were married and I think the wedding was what I had planned and dreamed about. The wedding photos at least seemed to verify that.

The honeymoon was short — one day of relaxation, sort of. Not the stuff that movies are made of because two days later, at 8:30 am, George pulled down the street and I tooted the horn to indicate I was behind him. It was our last communication for hours. But I prayed, "Please let the car keep going! Please let him know I'll need a washroom soon."

We drove over the Patullo Bridge. In 1952 it was not too busy. The cars became fewer until we reached Chilliwack and the dreaded five-way intersection. I kept my eyes glued to the back of our trailer, following closely behind George and made it through. I was grateful for a bathroom break and a chance to relax over coffee. We were off again, heading for Hope. As another section of the journey was completed there was another encouraging talk, and we were on our way again.

We made it to Cache Creek by 4 p.m. Tension turned to the shakes as I crawled out of the Buick in a motel parking lot. George helped me into our room and I was rejuvenated with a shower. At dinner he proudly informed me that I had driven the dreaded Fraser Canyon road. George's timing is good. I had little time to mull this over before I fell asleep that night.

The next morning we drove off, surrounded by ranchlands as we slowly climbed a long hill, then down the long slope across the valley. The descent was worrying because George needed to brake frequently and I had to pay close attention. I doubted he would appreciate the odd bump as I enjoyed the landscape.

After we passed Lac La Hache, we dropped off the end of the highway. Well it seemed like that; the road became gravel, and only had passing lanes on the hills. Finally we reached Quesnel after a long, stressful day.

Before we started out on the third morning George told me our destination was now within reach and we would be there around noon. So why was George turning on to this very bumpy, narrow track, I howled? The trailer was bouncing around in front of me, I was dodging rocks and potholes, the dust was blinding and all I could do was hang on to the wheel and keep my eyes glued straight ahead.

Finally George pulled over into a clearing, his brake lights came on and he stopped. He jumped out of the truck and ran over to hug me as I got stiffly out of the car. He was energized at the thought of building a road through the wilderness.

I was appalled at the outdoor toilet facilities.

He saw the opportunity to open the area for the development of forest resources.

I saw my bare arm attacked by bugs that surely weren't mere mosquitoes!

But, the next morning I awoke to sunshine and the smell of cooking bacon. My bridegroom offered to help unload our things from the truck and by noon we had company.

I guessed I would stay. I was excited about setting up our first home and I certainly was not going to drive that road again.

$48.50

By Sue Whittaker

Jane's marriage to Leonard foundered in the first six months of its pitiable existence. Unfortunately it dragged on for the next twenty-four and a half years. The man she had chosen to facilitate her escape from a hellish life in her parents' home was revealed to have no concept of generosity and was fixated on thrift. Every penny had to be accounted for or life was made unbearable. It became easier to do without and improvise than to endure the abuse that followed even the most paltry purchase that wasn't considered essential to life. There was one thing he did share, though, and shortly after the wedding, Jane found herself pregnant and totally dependent at the age of eighteen.

So, over two decades later, when Leonard died in a fit of recrimination over the unheard of expense Jane had incurred in the purchase of his high blood pressure medication, she took a deep breath and prepared to carry on. She was surprised to learn that there was enough money in her newly-accessible bank account to afford her a fairly comfortable lifestyle for as long as she expected to live.

"So Mom, what do you intend to do this winter?" her daughter Olivia prompted, six months after Leonard died.

"Well, I haven't thought about it," said Jane. "Stay home, keep warm, knit a sweater . . . or two?" she ventured bravely, "if I can get a good deal on some yarn. Why do you ask?"

"I thought maybe you might be ready to get out a bit more and meet some new people so I signed you up for a dance class that Matt and I are taking at the Rec Centre."

"Olivia! I haven't danced since before I was married. I can't do that!"

"Seems to me like you owe it to yourself to see if you can still shake your booty," Olivia teased. "Besides, there is this guy who works with Matt who wants to take the class but he needs a dance partner."

Jane *almost* contained a snort of disbelief. "I am sure a friend of Matt's would have no desire to be stuck with a woman my age who hasn't danced in twenty-five years. Don't be ridiculous, Olivia!"

"No, Mom, you don't understand. He's Matt's boss and he *is* your age and a bit more."

"How much more?" asked Jane, suspiciously.

"Come on Mom. Give it a try. You'll have fun, get some exercise and meet some interesting people."

"How much will these lessons cost?" Jane's voice quavered.

"Not a penny, Mom. Consider it an early Christmas present from Matt and me." Olivia could see her mom beginning to come around. She threw in a clincher: "And don't worry about what you're going to wear. I have us booked for a spa treatment the Saturday before classes start and we're going shopping together afterwards. Also, my treat."

"Well, my goodness," gasped Jane. "you have this all planned, don't you? A spa treatment and a new frock! That will set you back a few dollars."

"Not a problem, Mom. My decorating business is making an obscene amount of money these days with all the condo construction that's going on. I can afford it. When I think of how little you spent on yourself all those years Dad was alive so that I could have decent clothes to wear to school, I think it's payback time."

On the Thanksgiving weekend, Olivia picked her mom up at 7 am and they set out for "Garden of Delights," Olivia's favourite spa. Jane had a sinking feeling as they entered the premises. This was not her kind of place. She was swamped by Greek columns, candlelight, soft music, perfumed air, silk fabrics and beautiful estheticians gliding in and out of treatment rooms. And, oh my goodness! Who was that approaching her, smiling in a way no man had ever smiled at her in living memory?

"I'm Zack," he introduced himself. "Come with me Jane, I am your masseur today."

The mind-boggling experience of peeling down to her skivvies in order to allow a handsome stranger to turn her muscles to jelly, was followed by a full body apricot seaweed wrap, a facial, a manicure and a pedicure with a hot wax treatment. Entering another area of "Garden of Delights," Jane showered, was given a shampoo, a hair cut with highlighting and a professional make-up consultation. Olivia handed her a small bag of exquisite little jars of make-up and a bottle of perfume, the scent of which she had commented on throughout the day.

Then they were ushered into a small consulting room to have their chakras balanced. Jane was pretty skeptical about that whole procedure and didn't know whether she wanted to be responsible for the continuance of such a questionable therapy, alternative or not.

"Olivia," Jane gasped, scandalized by the mounting cost. "We can't possibly go shopping after all that!"

"It's okay, Mom. We'll just drop into this one little shop I love. They have put aside some things I scouted out for us yesterday after work. It will only take a few minutes to try them on. Then we'll meet Matt for a drink and supper at my favourite restaurant. You must be starved."

As Olivia was rushing to expedite the credit card transaction before her mom joined her from the change room, she added up what her day with her mom had cost. Even she was a bit daunted by the combined costs of the spa and their whirlwind shopping spree. Four thousand, eight hundred, fifty dollars and change, she calculated.

Jane had a set look to her face when she joined Olivia at the service counter. "I insist on paying my share today, Olivia. I am not poor, you know. Your father left me very comfortably off when he died. Even though the tags have been removed from everything I tried on, I know clothes are expensive in this shop. So tell me, and I *will* know if you are fibbing. What did this whole day cost you?"

"Come on Mom, I said this was my treat," Olivia whined.

"Don't try that with me, Olivia May! What is the damage?" she insisted, digging into her pocketbook.

"Okay Mom. Forty-eight fifty."

"Well, my goodness! I would have thought that last dress alone would have been worth at least fifty dollars! Here are two twenties and five toonies. You keep the change."

Mom's idea of high finance, Olivia thought, barely managing to keep a straight face.

Losing My Self

By Maureen Kresfelder

July 27, 2002

The truth is I don't want to write about it. But I must. I promised my daughter I would keep a journal of my thoughts and feelings about this insidious disease. She will publish it after — after I'm dead? Or after I'm totally demented? She will pass it on to other Alzheimer families. To help them, she says. It hurts me to know that I may have passed my defective genes on to her. I have Familial Alzheimer's. She must already be worrying and wondering if she will inherit this disease — she has a 50/50 chance. Wondering if she too, will be writing a journal at the behest of her children.

Alzheimer Disease is a progressive, neurodegenerative disease that destroys brain cells…. Gradually independence is lost. Alzheimer Society, British Columbia

My name is Patricia Kearney. I am 63. I am a retired English teacher. I have Alzheimer Disease. I can say it now, out loud, and accept it. When I was first diagnosed with it in June I refused to believe it. Not me, I said. I have always been mentally active. I have eaten a healthy diet for years. I take vitamins conscientiously. I exercise. I have an 89-year-old mother who is mentally competent. I cannot possibly have it. But I do.

Though I am no longer in denial I often feel terrified of what's ahead. Then I get angry and finally, exhausted by those emotions, depressed. I am working to accept those feelings too, as a normal reaction to a deadly disease. Hopefully, through acceptance, they will lessen.

164

I read about the disease voraciously as if confronting it in print will somehow alleviate the psychic pain of it, the fear of it, the despair. I am hoping secretly, fervently, that I will miraculously discover the doctors have made a mistake. But they have not.

In 1906, Alois Alzheimer, a German neuropatholgist and clinician, treated Auguste D., a 51 year old woman, for what was then termed "senility." He could not help her. When she died he performed a brain autopsy. He was the first to establish that at least one form of dementia had a biological basis and not a psychological one.

July 28, 2002

My name is Patricia Kearney. I still know who I am. I cherish the knowing. Someday I will not remember my own name let alone my history, my family or my friends. I'll be like Alois Alzheimer's patient, Auguste D. When interviewed by Alzheimer and asked to write her name she could only manage "Augu…" and then offered, "I have lost myself." I have not lost my self entirely, yet. And maybe, just maybe, the researchers will find a magic drug to stop this relentless deterioration of my brain. Oh god, I've done it again, become quite maudlin. But I am allowed to, aren't I?

Phoned my son, James. He erupted when I mentioned the "A" word. I will not phone him again. I cannot cope with his almost violent denials of my diagnosis. It's just too emotionally exhausting. There's so much I'd like to say to him about our relationship, especially now, but he is not ready to listen. Maybe all I need to say is "I love you," but he has trouble with the "L" word too. Especially since his marriage broke up.

July 30, 2002

My daughter, Elizabeth phoned. She asked if I had "remembered" to write about how I discovered I had Alzheimer's. "Don't worry, I said. "I've made a note of it — literally. There's a note on the fridge, a note on the bathroom mirror, and one on the computer desk." We both laughed. After we hung up I cried.

It had come to this: inundated with post-it-notes to remember what I used to "note" in my brain. I don't really want to think about the events leading up to the diagnosis, but I promised to leave a record. While I can.

Here's what happened: during March of this year, my husband, John, told me he noticed I had more frequent "senior moments." Often I struggled to find the right word. Occasionally, I completely forgot that I put laundry in to be washed or dried. And, I forgot to meet a friend for lunch, something I had never, ever done. "You seem scattered," he'd said. But he had memory lapses too, he added quickly. He asked if I thought "we" were just experiencing memory loss due to aging. I agreed with him, too eagerly it seems now, not wanting it to be anything else.

John was reassured and pleased when I bought a book on memory enhancement. "When something is wrong, you fix it," I said. He loved a "proactive wife." We set about using some of the memory improvement strategies. After little more than a week my memory seemed to improve somewhat (wishful thinking, perhaps?) and so did my husband's. We were proud of ourselves.

But two weeks later all hell broke loose. I got lost and terribly confused on the main street of Osoyoos! I didn't know whether to turn right or left at the traffic light to get to Super Valu. And then, when I did make the correct decision and found my way there I could not remember why I was there. My heart was thudding furiously. My mind was racing. I was terrified.

Something was terribly wrong with me. Calm down, I told myself, take a few deep breaths. You'll be all right. I rolled down the window to gulp in some fresh air. A woman came up to the window, greeted me and said, "Come over for coffee when you're finished shopping. I want to show you my dress for the wedding." I knew that I should know her. But I couldn't remember her name or where she lived. I muttered something about having a dentist appointment, rudely turned on the ignition and sped away. I don't remember how I got home.

That was Black Monday. The day that fear engulfed me, the day I curled up in the fetal position on the couch and couldn't speak to my husband until he threatened to call 911. I uncurled myself, sat up and wrapped my arms around my chest. I told him everything that had happened to me that day –- the horrible confusion, the unmitigated fear. I told him how worried I was about losing my mind. When I'd finished he just held me for the longest time. He reassured me over and over that we would get to the bottom of this, that there had to be a simple explanation. Then he phoned the doctor and said it was urgent. Just remembering that has drained me emotionally. Brought fresh tears. I can't go on right now.

The doctor selects appropriate tests for his patient. Although the test results may indicate Alzheimer Disease only a brain autopsy can give a definitive diagnosis. However, doctors' diagnoses have been accurate more than 90% of the time.

August 1, 2002

Awoke early this morning frightened, heart racing, panic-stricken –- from a nightmare. I had been trapped in a dark cave. The only light came from a narrow opening in the roof, far above. I tried to scale the walls. They were slippery –- I could get no foothold, no handhold. Just when I had resigned myself to waiting for rescue, the walls began to cave in. Slowly but surely I was being entombed by hundreds of pieces of falling rock. I screamed. And woke up. I was drenched in sweat and consumed with fear. I am now haunted day and night by this disease.

But before I forget, let me continue with yesterday's story. The next day, after "Black Monday," John and I went to see the doctor. I told him everything that had happened recently to cause me concern. John told the doctor his account of my behaviour in the last few months. He had noticed more out-of-character behaviour than I realized, like telling him the same bit of news two or three times in one day, or getting confused when adding up the grocery bills. The doctor did not dismiss our accounts as simply the result of "getting older." He immediately set about making appointments for a complete physical and blood work, an EEG, a CAT scan and appointments with a neurologist and psychologist. He said my symptoms could be caused by any number of physical conditions and diseases. He intended to find out what was causing them as fast as possible.

"As fast as possible," took a good 3 months. Agonizing months. And during that time the disorientation I had experienced on Main Street occurred several more times on my way to the library, the drugstore, the optometrist's, all once familiar routes.

In spite of my apprehension, I was still hopeful. Surely whatever was causing my brain cells to misfire must be treatable. I had steadfastly refused to even consider Alzheimer Disease; no one on either side of my family had ever had it, as far as I knew. Thus, I confidently reasoned, I couldn't have it. Could I?

On June 30, 2002 Dr. Freiburg, the neurologist, met with us to discuss the results of the testing. I was tense and anxious but expectant that I would soon be treated and cured. But my heart sank when the doctor pulled up his chair beside mine and held my hands. I knew then, with certainty — I had a deadly disease.

Gently, he said, "The results of the tests indicate that you have "probable" Alzheimer Disease. It is a progressive brain disease. I am going to put you on a drug that will help you to remain as mentally sharp as possible for as long as possible. There is a support group in town. You will want to join it."

I sat stunned. My mind raced to cope with the news. I could barely breathe. I jumped up and cried, "I don't believe it," and ran from the office and out to the car. John joined me minutes later and held me as I wept. When my flood of tears had subsided, I said morosely, "What now?"

"Dr. Freiburg said he would see us together again tomorrow. Then we can ask questions about this diagnosis. Find out what to expect, how to fight it."

"I know what to expect," I said bitterly, "a death sentence. How do you fight a death sentence?"

The drugs Aricept and Exelon are most often prescribed for Alzheimer Disease. The can inhibit the symptoms of Alzheimer's for a year or more. They do not slow the progression of the disease. They have side effects.

August 3, 2002

This morning I got up and forgot for a few minutes that I had Alzheimer's. Perhaps forgetting has its advantages, I thought grimly. I said that jokingly to my husband. He looked pained. He came over and gave me a tender hug.

"Maybe you don't have it," he implored, "maybe those doctors are guessing, just grasping at straws. You've been under a lot of stress with the family this last year." (Our daughter had had a miscarriage, our son and his wife had filed for divorce and were fighting over custody of their children.) "Stress can cause forgetfulness and confusion."

"We've been through that, John. And all the other possibilities. It's not stress, or mini strokes or medications or depression or loss of hearing or vision."

I was so pleased that, without pausing, I had listed six possible causes of cognitive loss and confusion. I was so happy to list those without going blank. I smiled delightedly.

"See, that's what I mean; you sound so normal," he said.

My smile faded. My voice rose tremulously. "John, I am normal. A normal person with a deadly disease. For God's sake, let me take pleasure in my small victories."

John is still in denial. He said he had come to terms with it. But he has not. He's irritable with himself and me. He broods. He tears when he thinks no one is looking. He's angry and frustrated with the doctors who can only prescribe drugs that ostensibly give more months of "quality life" for the patient — and their families. He is angry and devastated that he is losing me. And that I will some day lose all memory of him, and us. I too, grieve those future losses. But in time, only he will know what we've lost. I'm the lucky one then, am I?

Most Alzheimer patients eventually require round the clock nursing care. Nursing Home beds usually have to be reserved. Family members often delay their search because of feelings of guilt.

August 5, 2002

Elizabeth phoned to ask me how I was and how the journal writing was coming. I told her that my "better quality of life drug" was making me nauseous and giving me diarrhea, and that I would be switching to another that I may be able to tolerate better. But on the positive side, I felt mentally alert today. Not like some days when my brain felt "foggy." I told her that I would write about the family meeting we called to discuss the diagnosis. "Be honest," she said. "Tell how hard it was for James to accept it. That Grandma wouldn't come. And how the family could not face making arrangements for the future."

The family meeting was revelatory. We called it in mid-July to tell James and Elizabeth and her husband more about the diagnosis and what to expect. We did not invite our grandkids. They would have to hear it from their parents. My mother said she couldn't believe it and couldn't handle such a discussion. She did not attend.

Our children live in distant towns. We hadn't been together since Christmas. They had been unaware that anything was wrong. I'd managed to cover up my bloopers on the phone. I'd made jokes about memory and aging.

John had phoned the kids and told them the diagnosis the day after we heard. I had phoned my mother with the news. The hardest thing I'd ever done. She sobbed on the phone and said over and over, "I'm sure the doctors are wrong."

John and I chaired the family meeting. Whenever I got emotional, he took over until I had composed myself. I told the kids what to expect. I asked for their patience and understanding when I forgot something or got confused or moody and when, eventually, I would even forget their names. I told them I needed their love and support. John told them I would reach plateaus where there was no apparent further deterioration, and then I would get a little worse, and then plateau again.

My son would not accept it. He lost his temper and said the doctors were crazy. He insisted I get a second opinion. I told him I had. "Well, get a third, damn it!" Then he apologized shamefacedly and said, "Mother, doctors do make mistakes, you know. They're not infallible." My daughter asked if she should move back home to help out.

"Not yet," I said, "Dad will let you know if he needs help. But you all must promise me that long before I become a burden and can no longer toilet myself, or begin to wander off, or frequently forget who you are or who I am, you will let me move into a nursing home. This you must promise." Silence.

"John, say something."

"I haven't agreed to that. That's a hell of a thing to ask me to commit to. You want me to abandon you!"

They would not promise just then. The reality was still too new, too raw. I would have to try again later. But how much later? Would I remember? Would I care?

"Well, at least read about it," I said.

I gave them an Alzheimer's reading list. And referred them to several Alzheimer's web sites. I was back in teacher mode again, my daughter teased. I wanted them to know what they could expect in all stages of the disease. I wanted them to read about the stories of other persons' AD and the testimonies of caregivers. I wanted them to gain some insight into their own emotional reactions. I told them their father had power of attorney. I gave them copies of my will. My son walked out.

August 7, 2002

Phoned my mother today. She said she was coming up to see me. She was sure she would find I was wrong about that "Alzheimer's thing." "You're too young, besides," she said yet again, as if that erased the test results and the symptoms. A motherly reaction. I love her for it. When she's here, she'll notice the difference in me no matter how hard I try to be "normal." The visit will be hard on both of us.

Today I read a magazine article on Alzheimer's which concluded with the writer saying, "There but for the grace of God go I." What a horrible expression. Why on earth would anyone believe in a god that would grace some people and not others? Surely their god is more empathetic than that!

Speaking of God, my Baptist brother e-mailed and said he was praying for me. I have always believed in the power of prayer even though I do not embrace any religion. My spiritual belief, in a powerful energy force of love and healing, is still intact. I do not forsake my beliefs because of my disease. I just wonder why prayers are answered for some and not for others. The answer to that mystery is, more than ever, poignantly elusive. I e-mailed my brother and thanked him for his prayers, his kindness. I need all the prayers I can get, I told him. I'm praying too.

Love it when I use words like poignantly. Quality words have not been as forthcoming as they once were.

There are roughly three stages of Alzheimer's, early, middle and late. The length of time and the frequency with which the symptoms are expressed and the order in which they develop will differ from one patient to another. The early stage lasts about 2-3 years. One of the symptoms of early and middle stage Alzheimer is mood shifts and depression.

August 10, 2002

I couldn't write last night. By the end of the day I had spiraled down into a black abyss. I did not want to record effects of this disease on my life. I did not want to face it. I did not want to be reminded about the forgetting, the occasional confusion, the mental decline. Yesterday morning I found my place mats in the pot drawer. And I did not remember that our cat was at the vet's. I spent at least 30 minutes looking for her, calling her and then felt mortified when the vet phoned and said Mitzi was ready for pick up.

The books are right again. Your short term memory is the first to go. Why hadn't I written a Mitzi post-it-note? I'm so glad John was away golfing, had not been here to witness my "lapses," our euphemism for my mental deterioration.

I am now writing early morning. By the end of the day I am worn out by trying to be "normal," by fighting my "condition," another euphemism for my dying brain, coined by a well-meaning friend. Maybe I am already experiencing the "sundown syndrome" of AD patients. Caregivers in nursing homes find that their AD patients are often more competent, cooperative and amenable in the mornings. By late afternoon they become more confused and irascible. Why do I continue to read about my last days? To wallow in self-pity, I think.

I make a point of going to the gym in the a.m. too. My brain needs all the oxygen to the brain it can get. I am still driving. I don't often get disoriented in the morning. I seldom go out in the afternoons. My doctor has told me I may have to give up driving soon. John has just hinted at it knowing how distressing the idea is. I would be so dependent on him. Dependent. Makes me think of those ads for Depends, those adult diapers. That's in the late stage for some AD patients. The final ignominy. But I wouldn't know I was wearing them. That's a black blessing. And that's an oxymoron. Yes, I am showing off today with fancy words — why? It's proof to me that I haven't entered the next stage yet. What I haven't mentioned is that it has taken me an hour to dredge up *oxymoron* and *ignominy* even with the help of the thesaurus and John. And that I raged at my ineptitude.

John's patience is a marvel, although he can't keep the wounded look from his eyes.

August 13, 2002

The poet Dylan Thomas said, "Do not go gentle into that good night. Old age should burn and rave at close of day. Rage,

rage, against the dying of the light." But 63 is not even old age. Even though I rage occasionally, my anger has diminished. But then, so have I. I am diminished, smaller, less. As my memory fades and founders, so do I.

My son continues to rage steadily on my behalf. And his own I suspect.

I don't like to socialize much anymore. Too much pressure to sound normal. To pretend I'm handling it. Although I can be more relaxed around John and my two closest friends, I find I resent their normalcy from time to time. I'm not always easy to be around. And so sometimes, I hide, but then I can't stand the hiding. It seems so cowardly, so pathetic. Why don't I just tell family or friends I need some time for myself. My Self. Or will the irony make them blanch as it does me?

My mother arrived yesterday. Can't hide from her. Already I am emotionally spent. She began with, "If you fight this Alzheimer's thing it will go away." And, "You can beat it, I know you can." She told me to take Gingko, Vitamin E. She told me to try oxygen therapy. She said I must go to a naturopath. I tried to explain that there is no cure, that to date no Alzheimer patient had escaped no matter what the patient had tried. She balked at that, and argued, "We just haven't heard about those who beat it." I finally yelled ferociously, "You are in denial, Mother! Because you love me, because you don't want me to die. But the reality is that I may very well be dead or at least brain dead while you are still alive. I…can…not…stop…this…awful…disease!" and then proceeded to cry convulsively, uncontrollably. She came over and put her trembling arms around me. She comforted me as if I were her small child again. A portent of things to come?

I never realized how hard dying can be.

August 16, 2002

My mother left yesterday, tearful and chastened at the effects of this disease on her daughter. My monarchist mother was horrified when I couldn't remember the name of Prince Charles' wife. Or how old Queen Elizabeth was. Or where I was when Princess Diana died. She is in mourning already.

I went to my Alzheimer's support group. I needed it desperately. I told them about my mother's traumatic visit. They all empathized with the experience.

Every Wednesday morning we meet for an hour, sometimes two, and just talk about the frustration, the despair we feel about our mental decline. We talk about our hopes and fears for the future. We discuss our relationships with family and friends that have been so severely tested by this disease. We always end with jokes or funny stories about our illness despite one member's objection that Alzheimer's is no laughing matter. Laughter is cathartic, we tell her. "What does that mean?" the former nurse asks. We look at her aghast. Cathartic just means therapeutic we say, averting our eyes.

Weeks ago we even considered how we could help ourselves — after all, we are still in the early stages of the disease. We wanted to take charge of our lives for as long as we could. We compiled some strategies for coping. They include useful things like: using post-it-notes, keeping a day planner for appointments, carrying our name, address and phone number in our wallet to get help when we become confused, telling people when we can't follow a conversation completely, phoning each other for comfort and support, exercising regularly, and enrolling with the Alzheimer Wandering Registry — just in case. A group member typed up the complete list and ran it off on rose-coloured paper —a symbol of hope. I don't think we really believed, just then, that our symptoms would get any worse.

August 18, 2002

Read recently that Charlton Heston has Alzheimer's. He who played Moses in the Ten Commandments and parted the Red Sea. He who played Ben-Hur, super hero. I am certain that none of those dramas prepared him for this one. Will his Christian God come to his rescue now? Or will he rationalize his progressive decline into oblivion by saying that God works in mysterious ways or that it's God's will? Two more awful, awful expressions. How they belittle our intelligence and trivialize our anguish.

Heston prepared a taped statement for his fans. He wanted to tell them how much he appreciated them while he still could. I like his style. I admire his courage. His gun politics, however, appall me. But now that he has the Alzheimer's gun to his head, I feel only sympathy for him.

August 25, 2002

I did not write this past week. Why? Severely depressed. Just now "surfacing." Thank god for anti-depressants and John's support. He had the wit to ask if something more had happened that led to my depression. And something had. I had listened to the taped story of Thomas deBaggio, an Alzheimer patient. I identified with his anxieties, his terror, his loneliness and his obsessive need to dwell on his disease. And my disease became, quite simply, unbearable. For the first time in my life I contemplated suicide.

The optimism and sense of control our support group felt was short-lived. For the last two Wednesdays, Marie had not attended our meetings. I phoned her. Her daughter answered. She told me her mother had become paranoid about some members of our group. She thought they were plotting to steal her purse — she could never remember where she put it. But "worst of all," Marie had made a gross sexual pass at her minister, on Sunday — in public. She had scandalized the congregation. When I related that last bit of news we laughed till we cried. Then we became very quiet. She was the first to leave the group. Who would be next?

August 30, 2002

Writing this journal has become a burden. I do it now, as I do the treadmill, because I should.

Today I am having difficulty typing this. I have to go back and correct many words. Even spell-check is having a hard time

176

sorting out what I mean. My fingers won't always go where I want them too. I, who used to type 60 words a minute. John has suggested I dictate my journal and he type. I declined. How can I speak candidly with John sitting beside me? My story would be influenced by his presence, his expectations, his emotions. Tears again. I am so tired of them.

The official flower of the Alzheimer Society is the forget-me-not. It has a special meaning for me. Those are the words my father had engraved on my mother's wedding ring. A foreshadowing of his own early death and his daughter's? My father, perhaps the carrier of the Alzheimer genes, died in the Second World War. I will die in the Alzheimer War. Unless the scientists develop some ammunition to fight it, destroy it. Soon.

September 3, 2002

Today, everyone in our Wednesday support group was abuzz with the latest Alzheimer's news. "Scientists are experimenting with shunts." "They drain fluid from the patient's head." "Some patients' conditions stabilized." But then we realized the scientists will need at least two more years to complete their research. By then it will be too late for most of us.

"But maybe our kids will benefit," says George who is unfailingly optimistic.

"What about us?" snapped Nancy. "We want to live too."

As always, Nancy expresses what the rest of us think and feel but dare not say. Her bluntness is refreshing. We clap. As the meeting breaks up we realize that George is crying. We converge on him and give him a group hug.

I realize too, that I shall not meet with this group much longer. It is time for me to move on. I don't want to leave the way Marie did. I feel an inner calm for the first time since my diagnosis. Maybe it's because I accept it and am doing what I can to manage this disease. I have even made application to enter an Alzheimer care facility in two years' time. I told John we would still be able to spend a lot of time together. And that I expect conjugal visits. He didn't even smile. It was only after I pleaded with him to honour my decision and said, "I think I should be able to choose how and where I end my days," that he reluctantly agreed to make the reservation with me.

Also, I have decided what I want to do with the rest of my "early stage" time. I will write letters, letters to my "fans" à la Heston. I will write an appreciation letter to my husband, my kids and grandkids, my mother, my brother and my two dearest friends. That's how I want to spend my remaining time. I want to tell them what they have meant to me — while I still can. And I want to visit with them as much as their schedules allow. I'll take the Greyhound.

For me, "memory time" is of the essence. So Elizabeth, I am done with this journal. But I am definitely not done with life. And, I will always be hoping for a miracle. Even though my disintegrating brain and my battered heart tell me it will not come.

The Night I met Jimmy Buffett

By Jody Chadderton

"Let me tell you about the night I met my friend, Jimmy Buffett."

"You know Jimmy Buffett?"

"Well, not exactly. I met him in a dream. But I'd really like to meet him. I feel like I'm already in love with him, like maybe we're soul mates."

"The only thing I have in common with Jimmy Buffett is that we were both born the same year."

"Actually, Dad, that's not Jimmy Buffett. You're talking about his older brother, Warren." I know I've mentioned Jimmy Buffett to Dad before, and he always confuses my favourite folk singer with the CEO of Berkshire-Hathaway, who is currently ranked as the third richest man in the world.

"Yeah, Warren Buffett, that's who I meant. We were both born in 1930."

"Only we weren't talking about Warren Buffett."

"I was."

"Dad, I was going to tell you about the night I met Jimmy Buffett."

"Only you didn't really meet him. Is he really Warren Buffett's brother?"

"I made that up."

"You made up the whole thing. Why do I listen to you?" He folded his arms across his chest and looked away, pretending he was through listening to me. We had been bantering like this long enough for me to know that the conversation was far from over.

"It's amusing , Dad. Hear me out, okay?" He turned back and nodded, so I continued. "I should set the scene first. Do you have any tequila? Okay, rum and coke then. I can mix drinks while I tell you the story. You know that song 'wasted away again in Margaritaville. . ?'" I actually tried to sing a few lines and Dad didn't laugh, but I'm not sure he recognized the song from my inept rendition. "It's always been a favourite of mine, especially since learning to drink tequila in Mazatlan. When I was seventeen, remember? So, I heard that song and, in typical teenage fashion, I got the words wrong and I thought he was searching for a lost acre of song. Okay, it didn't make sense, but I sang it anyway. I really liked the song a lot better when I finally learned about the lost shaker of salt. And I felt very sophisticated because I had actually learned to drink tequila shots with a lick of salt and a wedge of lime. It took me a while to catch what he was saying, but when my ear caught it, yeah, it made sense. But that's not when I fell in love." I handed Dad his drink and we clinked our glasses.

"A couple years ago when Pete and I were in Las Vegas I browsed in the gift shop of the Margaritaville Restaurant. They sell souvenir T-shirts with bits of song lyrics and shot glasses and sets of Margarita glasses with a pitcher and cool patio chairs and CD's of his music. And to my surprise I discovered he had also written a couple books. For some reason all I did was browse, but when we returned to Vegas this year, I went back to the shop determined to buy a CD. I thought it would be a fun addition to my next Cinco de Mayo party."

"You didn't have a party this year."

"No, but that's another story. Remember last year I was scrambling to find music that sounded Mexican or Latin or Spanish? So this time I figured we'd have Jimmy Buffett. Not classic Mexican, but a variation on the party theme. I even thought about buying goofy hats that looked like parrots because Buffett fans are called Parrot-Heads, but I didn't. I bought this

2-CD set which has all his greatest hits, including of course Margaritaville, and I also bought his novel.

"I hate to say this, but I wasn't expecting much. Celebrities sometimes get published on the basis of their fame rather than their literary talent. Well, I started reading the novel in the airport, continued on the plane, and by the time we landed I was well on my way to falling in love. And that was before I listened to his two CD's about a hundred times in a row. He is part pirate, part cowboy, part novelist and, of course, a brilliant folk singer. His lyrics and his characters are so full of humour and quirkiness. I just want to stalk him and give him a big hug and maybe stay up all night drinking tequila with him. In one of his songs he mentions he goes for younger women. Do you think I have a chance?"

"Well you might if you actually got to meet him. In the flesh, that is. Also, you already have Peter, or have you forgotten? I thought you had decided Peter was your soul mate. So is that the dream, you stalk Jimmy Buffett and you stay up all night drinking tequila together?"

"Don't laugh, Dad, that's pretty much it. In the dream, I find his concert schedule on-line, and I fly to Cincinnati and get a ticket to his concert. It's an outdoor concert with open seating and I push through the crowd to get right up close to the stage with a bunch of screaming teenagers. Some of the girls look so young, maybe they're not even teenagers, but the way they are dressed makes me think their mothers wouldn't be proud. This season's version of sexy, I suppose. I must look so out of place in my long hippy dress and sandals with a wilted flower in my hair, but I can't help wanting to be there. The kids are making fun of me, but I try to ignore them. When Jimmy comes on stage, he sees me, and he seems to be singing directly to me. His words go right through me and I feel like I'm going to faint, but there's no room to fall anyway because everyone is crammed so tight. All these very young, very slutty-looking girls swaying to music they've probably never heard before. One of Jimmy's songs, 'The Last Mango in Paris. . . .'"

"Did you say 'mango'?"

"Yup, it always makes me want to cry when I hear it, and when he sings it to me at the concert it suddenly makes perfect sense (although when I wake up I don't remember the meaning.) After the concert, I'm standing in front of the stage with tears soaking the front of my dress and the crowd is starting to disperse and one of the stage hands sees me and winks and the next thing I know Jimmy Buffett is back on stage and he reaches down and pulls me up to his level. He is taller and larger than I expected and his arms feel deliciously strong. He introduces himself as if we've just met in a bar. Then I introduce myself and he says 'the writer?' and he acts like he's as thrilled to finally meet me as I am to meet him. He says he's read all my books, and I say I've read all his." I wink at my dad and say, "Don't forget this is a dream."

"Anyway, next he takes my hand and says we're going down to Captain Tony's, which is the setting of one of the songs I really love. You know how in a dream you open the door and you're not in Kansas (or, in this case, Ohio) anymore? We walked into Captain Tony's — I don't know how we got there — and it's like a tropical paradise, something from Hawaii or the Caribbean, or maybe Key West. The light is dim inside in contrast to the scorching sun and the air is stirred by ceiling fans. He leads me to a table for two, one of those wicker bistro tables, and he clasps both my hands in his across the table as we stare into each others' eyes talking about music and writing and, believe it or not, baseball. Jimmy is a huge baseball fan and his head is full of obscure stats. At least one of his songs has a baseball theme, and baseball is featured in his novel. I am such a sucker for baseball in stories. It might be cliché, but it's a metaphor for life. George Bowering is also a baseball fan who has written stories and poems about baseball, and, when I mentioned him, Jimmy said he liked his writing too. Can you imagine? I know he's a smart guy and probably well-read, but I hardly expected Jimmy Buffett to have heard of many Canadian writers, let alone read any.

"Meanwhile, the Coral Reefers are in one corner playing a familiar Calypso rhythm. Jimmy nods at the waiter who brings over a couple shots of tequila with lime. Jimmy has to search the other tables for our missing salt shaker, and we both laugh so hard my eyes start watering again. He wipes my tears away with his thumb and the gesture is so tender I can't stop. That's when he lifts me from my chair and gives me a warm hug and then his lips brush my eyelids and with my eyes closed I feel for a moment like we're the only ones in the bar."

"If this is a sex scene coming up I don't want to hear it." Wearing a silly grin, Dad puts his hands up to cover his ears.

"No, it's more like a cuddle scene. He sits back down and pulls me onto his lap. His strong sailor arms surround me. I guess he's nodded again to the waiter because there's another two shots of tequila, but the salt shaker is missing again. This time he doesn't bother to search for it. We take turns pouring tequila into each others' mouths, spilling Cuervo down the front of our clothes and laughing. Even sticky and wet, I feel so incredibly comfortable with him like I've known him forever. We share a few more shots of tequila, which have just magically appeared on the table. There's no awkwardness, no hesitation."

Dad urges me on: "How does it end?"

"His horse Mr. Twain is waiting outside the bar and he pulls me up behind him on the horse and we ride down the beach, me with my arms around his waist of course, hanging on a bit tighter than necessary. Then we see this old-fashioned schooner, just like the Bluenose on the tail of our dime, anchored in the harbour. He says he has to leave and asks me to come with him. I'm thinking: whisk me away from my humdrum existence to a new life of sailing and fishing and concert tours and whatever. Who cares, as long as it includes Jimmy Buffett. And then I remember Peter, and I'm feeling guilty even thinking about leaving. I don't even know Jimmy, even though I'm almost convinced that he's

Mr. Right. I once thought that about Pete — was that only yesterday? What is it about Jimmy? Is he so different from Peter or so much like him? I wished I had more time, more time to spend with Jimmy, more time to make a decision.

"I don't know if I'm making the biggest mistake of my life, but I tell him no. We hug and grope and as I'm kissing him I'm thinking about changing my mind. But then I slide off the horse and turn back up the beach and walk away."

"That's it?"

I shook my head. "You know at the end of a movie when the hero or heroine suddenly turns around and comes running back? It was like that, but I was too late. I came running back down the beach kind of in slow motion like I'm running through water and he was waving to me from the schooner. I thought, how'd you get there so fast? And then I wondered if I was maybe just too slow. So I stood on the beach and waved with tears streaming down my face."

Mothers of the Bird Kind

By Maureen Olson

A persistent "chit-chit, chit-chit," drew my attention from the book club novel I was struggling with. I looked up to see a female kingfisher sitting on the top of a blown-down tree at the water's edge. My eye was then drawn to, what was probably her active chick, as it dove repeatedly from a branch in an attempt, I surmised, to catch a fish.

Up it would come, checking with Mom for guidance, then down it would go, again and again. Each time, on its return to the branch, Mom would chatter instructions, with a final strident chirp for good luck.

Keeping my eye on things as I persevered with the novel, I observed a surprised chick surface from the lake with a two-inch fish caught in its beak.

It looked at Mom. I could almost hear the chick say, "What do I do now?"

Mom replied with a series of "Chit-chit-chit-chit?" Well Done!

A kingfisher, the chick had become.

I felt privileged to have witnessed the transition.

One spring morning while checking my garden, a chirping sound drew my attention to the 30-foot pine tree up the slope from me. We had noticed a large stick-loaded untidy nest nearly at the top. Things were happening up there if you could go by the chirping emanating from the tree-top home.

I couldn't believe my eyes. I saw a wood duck waddling away from the base of the tree. She was followed by little balls of fluff, with little legs moving quickly. Then I saw a couple of balls of feathers floating down from the nest. As soon as they had fallen and touched the ground, their legs were pedaling to catch up with the first chicks. I watched as they progressed across the yard, about 200 feet to the lake.

Mother quacked several times when she waddled into the water. As soon as they reached the water, the chicks started paddling even more quickly than they waddled. All of the family was soon out of my sight.

Some swimming lesson, I thought. It should have been so easy with my kids!

A Tale from a Marketplace

By Anita L. Trapler

I hold the doll, turning her around. She's exquisitely decorated with a gold tiara and filigree jewelery. Her cerulean eyes with their thick black eyelashes penetrate mine. Impossible. No, I think, Chinese people have been born with blue eyes. Why not a black child, like this black doll?

A woman stands near the table, gazing at the doll. "I met a girl in elementary school," she says. "I brought her home. My dad saw her. He flinched.

"After she left he said, 'Never bring that child into the house again. She's black and we don't mix with those people.'

"My eyes brimmed with tears. I said, 'Dad, please, just get to know her.'

"Dad remained tight-lipped. Silent. But his silence was my hope. Dad worked late nights at the milk plant, so Ariana often came home with me.

"We traded comics, played jacks and braided each others' hair," the woman continued. "We dressed up my rag dolls and a porcelain doll with Shirley Temple curls. I felt uneasy about Dad. If he saw Ariana again, would he shame us both?

"One stormy afternoon, Ariana and I were seated at the kitchen table when my dad walked in. We were drinking hot chocolate and dunking cookies.

"Dad hung his jacket behind the door and sat down. Ariana broke into an impish grin, poured him a cup of hot chocolate and passed the plate of cookies. She enchanted him.

"When Ariana tossed her raven hair, she might have passed for Indian or Mexican. But Ariana was Irish; a descendant of the Moors.

"It didn't matter.

"Ariana and I continued to be best friends. Dad gave her away on her wedding day. I served as matron of honour."

The lady at the marketplace then turns and begins to walk away.

"Wait!" I call.

I purchase the black doll and give it to her, saying, "Ariana will surely love this doll."

Leap of Faith

By Sue Whittaker

Clutching the edge of the kitchen sink, Lill rested her swollen belly against the cabinet below, as ripping pain cut through her lower back, leaving her breathless. The paring knife and potato dropped from her hands into a basin of water with a plop. The shrieks and laughter of her two snowbound youngsters gave her the focus she desperately needed to maintain consciousness. Breathe, breathe, she challenged herself, staving off a fainting spell, not the first she had experienced in the last week. But as the threatening wall of blackness and the ringing in her ears subsided, she was far too aware of the warm fluid puddling around her ankles.

Too soon, she thought. Please, not yet!

The next wrenching pain convinced her that her third child was definitely about to arrive, ready or not. A quick glance to her right assured her that her pride and joy, a gleaming new electric stove, a repossession they were paying off at two dollars a month, was turned off, and her iron was unplugged. No time to pack a bag, she regretted, as she changed from her sodden hose and underwear while imploring her five-year-old daughter to gather jackets, leggings, mittens and caps and help her brother get ready to go.

A call to the taxi service and another to her sister-in-law, Helene, got her a ride to the hospital and care for Lucy and Tommy.

The Consolidated Mining and Smelting Company was a paternalistic employer and Rossland a company town, but still not the employee-friendly organization that you would call in a moment of need. Her husband would not be available until his eight-hour shift was over. Maybe not even then if there was a chance that his drinking buddies might be meeting at the beer parlour after work. And there were those other unexplained absences from home as well. Lill had noticed they were becoming more frequent as her pregnancy advanced.

She was met by a nun with a wheelchair at the hospital steps. Helene must have called ahead to alert them as she organized packing up the kids to take them to her home.

Now she had only one responsibility, to birth this baby.

"Do not push!" scolded the Nursing Sister. "We must wait for the doctor to get here before we deliver this baby."

Panting heavily, and easing on to the side of her hip, Lill did her best to get control of the engine inside her that was pushing to the finish line. One did not challenge Sister Francis on medical matters.

As the wheelchair sped through the halls to the delivery room, it became more and more clear to Lill, who was after all, a veteran in child delivery, that the baby's head was knocking up against the door to the world.

But Sister Francis was adamant. Pulling towels off a shelf, she used them to hold the infant in place, determined to slow things down until the doctor got there. Sister's word was obeyed, but the doctor's word was law.

And the doctor was finishing his supper, wasn't he? Sister was quick to point out. They prayed he would forego dessert just this once, although it was well known he had a sweet tooth.

A live baby was delivered, in time. She was smallish and needed some help breathing at first but after a few days of respite for Lill, and another failed attempt at nursing, mother and child were released to go home.

Lill was plunged back into a life of late-night parties, a house filled with cigarette smoke, drunks, and noise. She dragged herself from bed many mornings to dispose of empties and cigarette butts before her three-year-old son got into them. A rising level of exhaustion claimed her days as anemia and worry dogged her.

But that was to be a hiatus, a break, before the storm in its real fury, broke over her head.

"Mommy!" her daughter screamed one Sunday morning after Lill's too few hours of sleep and a particularly rough Saturday night. "Mommy, wake up! Tommy is throwing up all over the walls! Come on, get up, I don't know what to do!"

Lill was unfamiliar with projectile vomiting but it was obvious her son needed medical help. Once more she was off to the hospital. And who knew when the Doctor would be available if he was a church-going man.

The diagnosis was, in the end, too soon in coming. Her son, Thomas Edwin had developed tumors throughout his abdomen that were growing at a prodigious rate. They would do an exploratory operation, more for the benefit of medical science than her son. She was convinced to allow the procedure when told that it might help other children down the road. There was no help for her son.

Farming out Lucy to her neighbour and the baby to her sister-in-law who was obviously overwhelmed with the care of a newborn, Lill virtually took up residence at the hospital. The long days and nights were made sadly sweet by Tommy's delight in having his mother all to himself and his apparent desire to learn every nursery rhyme he could in the time he had left. Lill would never hear *Oh, do you know the Muffin Man?* for the rest of her life, without succumbing to tears. When Tommy no longer had the strength to sing it himself, he could will her to sing it for him, forming "muffin man" with his lips and moving his fingers slightly, his signal that she should tap the rhythm on his palm.

Lill's husband, Reg, was unable to cope with the crisis. He rarely visited the hospital and hardly changed his lifestyle. The girlfriend, who Lill suspected had captured his interest, became a regular part of his life, a fact Lill's mother, Amy, did not hesitate to point out when she landed in the hospital not long after Tommy was admitted. A prolapsed uterus and newly diagnosed diabetes left Amy prone to collapsing. Lill found herself racing from the

Women's Ward to the Children's Ward and back again, as one catastrophe after another assailed her loved ones.

When Lill's son died in the spring of 1946 she was in need of loving attention herself. She barely remembered attending the funeral and without the keepsake program would not have known which hymns were sung, which psalms offered up on her son's behalf.

"I was floating above the proceedings and watching from the ceiling I was so heavily sedated," was all she recalled.

"No rest for the wicked, though," she would joke afterwards. Her baby came down with pneumonia, was hospitalized and living in a steam tent which Lill was sure would catch on fire from the hotplate that supplied the heat to generate the steam. Steam that was thought to be efficacious in these infant illnesses preceding the days of antibiotics.

Another long vigil ensued, and, as the baby recovered, it seemed to Lill that her daughter was not fully mobile. Although she moved her left foot and arm in the usual flailing motions of infants, her right side was suspiciously still.

When she eventually pointed these problems out to the doctor, he dismissed her concerns out of hand. "You are seeing things that are not there because of the loss of your son. This baby is fine. Take her home and enjoy her. Put this out of your mind."

And as much as Lill would have liked to do that, a one-sided baby did not sit well with her. As time progressed, Suzy was slow to walk and could not put her right heel down. Neither could she manipulate anything with her right hand, and she had very poor balance. Being a superb athlete herself, loving and excelling at every sport she had ever become involved in, Lill saw this handicap her daughter was struggling with as extremely restrictive and hard to bear.

Taking the opportunity to visit a traveling crippled children's clinic, to which her doctor refused to refer her daughter, she waited all one long, sad day for attention. The concern she felt for her daughter was eclipsed by the magnitude of the problems with which she saw other mothers coping.

In the early evening, when she and her daughter were the only ones left in the hall, a young, red-headed specialist, a Dr. Sparks, still managing a smile and a show of interest asked, "Do you have an appointment? You've been here a long time."

It had been hard to overlook the active little toddler who had played happily among the wheelchairs and grinned up at him every time he appeared to collect a new patient.

"No appointment," said Lill, "but I am sure there is something wrong with my daughter."

"Well, I never doubt a mother," he joked. "Bring her in."

The whole story of the birth came out in the examination room and it was confirmed that her daughter suffered from spastic paralysis, probably the result of oxygen deprivation at birth. There were some exercises that might lengthen the cord at the back of her leg, enabling her to put her heel down eventually and anything the child could do to involve and exercise the right hand would be beneficial.

Leaving the hospital with a sense of relief and vindication, but saddened to think of the activities Suzy was never going to be able to enjoy, Lill set her hand on her rounding tummy and wished for an uneventful delivery at the end of the summer. The myriad other problems in her life would be dealt with as needed.

The Royal Bank Epiphany

By Maureen Kresfelder

Our small bicycle business was losing money fast. And Caps, a bicycle chain store, had just opened another store nearby. What's more, the landlord of our bicycle shop had recently raised the rent. For two years we had barely broken even, my husband not able to draw a cent in wages. But now we were taking in less than our expenditures. Debt had entered the picture. That was not a part of our business plan.

As I walked over to the bank one rainy morning to deposit the meager money for yesterday's sales, I was lost in gloomy thought. I pictured us having to declare bankruptcy, take out a second mortgage, or simply sell the cozy old character house nestled in the hills that I had grown to love. Even though I had a job, my wage alone was not enough to sustain us much longer.

The line up in the bank was long. I had too much time to think about the bleak outlook for our business. We had invested our entire savings into this shop. And now we would likely lose it. My mood worsened. I could feel the tears welling up in my eyes. I would have to try and alter my mood quickly or leave the line up. Take a few deep breaths, I told myself. Chant some positive affirmations.

I breathed deeply and mentally affirmed, "I am calm, I am at one with the universe. I am calm. I am at one with the universe." And then it happened — I was flooded with love. Every cell in my body was suffused with love, vibrating with love — right there in the Royal Bank of Canada, small town British Columbia. From the top of my head to the tips of my toes, I was drenched in love. This sensation filled me and radiated within me for at least 10 seconds. And then it was gone, as mysteriously as it had come.

I don't remember making that meager deposit. I do remember leaving the bank awestruck, in a dream-like state. I did not tell my husband immediately what had happened. In fact, I didn't tell him for over a year. I couldn't – not only was the experience too spiritually intimate, I simply could not find the words. How could I ever tell anyone or explain what seemed to me an ineffable, profoundly spiritual experience.

But I did get the message: I was loved. And nothing else was as important as that. It was like someone or something was speaking to me telepathically through my very essence. But what was the something or someone, I wondered. Perhaps there was a scientific, medical explanation for my filled-with-love experience—like a tumour of the brain. Or maybe I had dementia. All highly improbable, of course. Perhaps, the phenomenon was my body's way of providing a healing, comforting response to mental distress. That seemed more plausible but still didn't feel right. Perhaps the experience was in response to my spiritual beliefs. Although I am not a traditionally religious person, I have always believed in some loving, powerful energy that can be drawn on and called upon. Maybe I somehow tapped into that source. That's the explanation that finally resonated with me. But I'll never know for sure. And it doesn't matter — for it will never change the "knowing" that came with the experience. Knowing that there is a universal force of love to which we are all connected.

Well, we didn't lose the business. And somehow, I just knew we wouldn't. Sales picked up. We paid our bills. My husband began drawing a substantial wage every month. We even managed to sell our bicycle business two years later for a modest profit.

"I still can't believe we sold our business for a profit," my husband said as he locked the door to the bicycle shop for the last time. "Must have been your guardian angel that helped us."

My husband believed we all had one and had interpreted my experience to fit his beliefs.

"I think you may have something there," I replied, quite willing to entertain that possibility too.

Ever since that epiphany I have felt calmer, handling the challenges and problems of my everyday life with greater equanimity. Every once in awhile, when I feel upset or feel a "poor-me" attitude coming on, I remind myself about my Royal Bank epiphany, as I have come to call it. Then I rein myself in and remind myself what that Royal Bank epiphany taught me: that love will help to bring you through the tough times. And that love, both given and received, is the quintessential meaning of life.

God Wot!

By Sue Whittaker

Every once in a while I just have to hear her voice again. That slightly husky quality, with the laugh sitting right on the edge, makes me feel sixteen years old as soon as I hear it.

I dial.

"Hello?"

"A Garden is a lovesome thing."

"God wot!" she laughs. "How you doin' Suzie Q?"

It's like a secret code, so obscure that there is probably no one else in the whole world who has the key. No one who would have been forced to memorize that bizarre little ten-line poem and still remembers it fifty years later.

Thomas Edward Brown wrote it over a hundred years ago, and Margie B and I think that we, in a population of over four billion, are probably the only ones left to delight in its Victorian tomfoolery. You see, we had this Welsh teacher in Grade Seven at the Kaslo School, the first Kaslo School, I should point out, not the second or third, made of huge blocks of granite and red brick, with oiled wood floors and real slate blackboards. There were transoms over the doors to each classroom, installed in the mistaken belief that they would help circulate air, keeping our classrooms cool in the heat and warm in the cold of winter. Inside each room, to the right or left of each door, was a separate cloakroom with a brass hook for each person's coat. Our desks had tops that flipped up, a great feature if one was suddenly overcome with the giggles, a condition best kept hidden from the teacher.

The ceilings were about 14-feet high with light fixtures that hung down and hummed all the time. The lower windows in the classroom opened by means of a winding device, and the upper transoms could only be accessed by a ten-foot pole with a brass wing digit on the end that clamped on to a brass fixture, allowing you to pull the transom open.

On the lowest floor, between the boys' and girls' washrooms, there was a boiler room with mammoth boilers and a coal-fired furnace. Years before, the man who would later be my father-in-law, stood at the edge of a pit and watched his father, and a crew of men, lower the whole business into the bottom of the construction site. He was three years old at the time, and it was his earliest childhood memory.

The ugly concrete basement activity room, with bars in the windows and a prevailing smell of burning coal, was the place into which we were marched first thing every morning throughout elementary school. We were lined up by class, exposed to a Bible reading, said The Lord's Prayer in unison and were expected to sing "God Save Our King" (which became "God Save Our Queen" in the middle of the year) in a heartfelt manner. Then The Roll Call was performed to which we were expected to answer, at the appropriate time, "Present!" All through Grade One I lived in hope that Christmas would come early to me, the kid with the biggest smile and the most tuneful reply. My older sister finally disabused me of that idea.

She rolled her eyes. "It's not that kind of 'present' you dope!"

This all happened before you took your coat and hat and boots off, in the winter. I still remember the smell of wet wool and sweat that rose off the student body and the sound of all those feet tramping up the stairs to our classrooms later — and NO TALKING either. Isn't it strange, I used to think, how they spend hours of our time in school teaching us to speak properly, but on the other hand, they hate to hear us in conversation.

Back to the Welsh teacher, Mr. Davies, who was in Kaslo for a one-year teacher exchange. It was his brilliant idea that our split class of Grade Seven and Eight students should memorize, with proper punctuation, that little gem of antiquity, the poem, "My Garden." We assumed it must have been written by a countryman of his, the importance he attached to it and all. So there it was as we took our places one morning, handwritten on the blackboard in his peculiar British script, (no McLean Method there).

My Garden

A Garden is a lovesome thing, God wot!
    Rose plot,
    Fringed pool,
    Ferned grot —
    The veriest school
    Of Peace; and yet the fool
Contends that God is not —
Not God! in Gardens! when the eve is
    cool?
Nay, but I have a sign:
'Tis very sure God walks in mine.

Thomas Edward Brown
(1830-1886)

Well, at first we balked. No way! What was the point! Who cares about his bloody garden? Who cares about any bloody garden when you're thirteen years old? It was bad enough we were forced to do hard labour in the family vegetable patch with all that attendant guilt attached after the war.

"The children in Europe would be glad to have fresh vegetables," we were told ad nauseam, "and furthermore, in the Depression . . ."

Here we go again, we thought, but we would have been slapped into the middle of next week if we had dared to say it.

So "My Garden" had several strikes against it. Only ten lines but we would have gladly memorized all thirteen stanzas of "Casey at the Bat" had we been given a choice. Like that ever happened! We're talking cricket and afternoon tea, here. Baseball was not even on the radar screen.

So, with great sighs and a lot of grumbling, we turned our thoughts to Mr. Brown's garden.

"A Garden is a lovesome thing." A Garden is a *lovesome* thing. What the heck did that mean? Who ever cuddled up in a pea patch? Furthermore, anybody who had picked corn had no love for that species.

Ah . . . but perhaps the reference was to cucumbers we would jest as we grew older and our fascination with that notable psychological concept, the phallic symbol, arose . . . and grew.

This whole "Garden" thing was straightened out for me when I was a teacher myself and someone explained that in Britain, the term "garden" referred to the flowers and lawn.

Got it!

Only ten years too late.

We called it "the yard," as in, "Mrs. Green has a beautiful front yard." Not "garden," right? Thank God we eventually developed our own body of literature here in Canada. The French might have a different word for everything, but the Brits aren't far behind!

So, on to "God *wot*." As I recall, we assumed that there had been a printing error, since our school dictionaries had no such word listed. So we "substituted the word *wrought* meaning, "beaten into shape with tools," but kept the easier of the two spellings. No sense in making things any more difficult, was there?

Then we tackled, "Fringed pool, ferned
grot —"

Well, who wanted to go there, I ask you? "Fringed pool"? Like Doukabour gumballs, we speculated? Those strings of dangling purple pompoms that boys strung around the ceiling of their souped-up cars? Those would look charming around a water feature —after a cloudburst or two.

And "ferned grot." Well, pee-eew! We used the word *grotty* to describe piles of dirty socks and sinks full of forgotten dishes. Why would you transfer this image to a garden you expected to go into ecstasies over? Wales sounded more and more like a country we might avoid should we ever graduate from Grade Seven and go on to be world travellers.

So . . . "the veriest school
Of Peace; and yet the fool
Contends that God is not —"

Well, there wasn't any doubt in our minds that somebody had screwed up on the placement of "Of Peace," and try to find *veriest* in a dictionary.

"And yet the fool Contends" struck a chord so we moved on to, "Not God!" (loved that exclamation point) "Not God!" we would sob, "in Gardens!" like gardens were next to Godliness.

I remember we used that line once, in a lamp post discussion we were having with fellow skeptics hanging around after Library night. At that time in our lives we were all Doubting Thomases but hadn't yet given up entirely on our Sunday School lessons.

"Not God!" Margie B howled.

"in Gardens!" I wept.

"when the eve is cool?" – together.

Our timing was faultless.

With smug looks on our faces, we delivered the *coup de grace.*

"Nay, but I have a sign:
'Tis very sure God walks in mine."

It was a small victory. You use what you have.

We still carry with us the memory of reciting Mr. Brown's masterpiece to each other as we trudged to school while we were learning it (punctuation included, little brats that we were!)

"A capital G garden is a lovesome thing comma capital G God wot exclamation point."

We had our lugubrious rendition in our Dief the Chief voice.

"A Garden (pause to reflect and get the jowls moving) is a Loooooovesome thing, (make meaningful eye contact) God . . . wwwoooot!" in the Voice of Doom.

That was our favourite, actually.

We can both still recite it at about one hundred miles an hour without taking a breath, which makes it even more incomprehensible than the original, which is going some.

After not having seen a copy of the poem since it appeared, unwanted, on the blackboard that morning, imagine my surprise, and yes, I admit, my delight, when I found it in a second-hand copy of *Bartlett's Familiar Quotations (1951 Edition)* that I had recently purchased. Of course I had to phone

Margie B.

I dial.

"Hello?"

"A garden is a lovesome thing."

"God wot," she laughs. "Can you believe we are still doing this?"

So I tell her about finding the *Bartlett's Familiar Quotations* containing Mr. Brown's opus.

"Bartlett," she pronounces, "seriously misnamed his book."

In the spirit of middle-aged good will and deeper understanding, we agree to give Mr. Brown his due. Anything that sticks with you that long must have some redeeming value.

Her Wish

By Maureen Olson

I was chosen to come to your house
    as your son's bride.
I came with a desire to learn.
Initially I accepted your demands with respect,
    so I could keep my pride, although your
    actions showed rejection of my attempts
    to do things your way.
So different from what I had learned.

I wish us to have an understanding of each other.

Is this what you experienced as a new bride?
    Feelings of rejection and sadness you kept
    hidden until now?
You make demands of me, hoping my subservience
    will make you stronger.
I can not return to my parental home, nor could you.

We are living in a new country, in a new society.
My husband expects more of me, he wants me to
    be a partner not a servant.

We will have harmony when we two can talk,
    to recognize one another's differences so
    there will be quiet, if not acceptance.

My Sister, the Valkyrie

By Sue Whittaker

In the grand scheme of things, I believe I was destined to join the League of Peacemakers on this earth. My sister, Bernice, was meant to carry the Battle-ax banner in the Grudge Match of Life.

Boadicea would have welcomed her on her left flank; Joan of Arc would have met a much kinder end had Bernice been her second-in-command. But instead, I got her for an older sister.

She was born seven years before I was, a child of World War II, while I was born into a world thirsting for peace. Unfortunately there was to be little harmony or accord in her vicinity, throughout our childhood.

And I was not the only one she took issue with on a daily basis. She could raise the hackles on my parents' necks with a mere look. She never hid her feelings, and she never backed down. And it made life a battleground in our home.

I have no pleasant memories of her from my childhood, and she probably carried just as few of me. She could terrorize me with a pillow feather and send me into shock by threatening me with the two "rats" that dwelt in a bureau drawer and had once adorned my grandmother's coat collar.

"Listen, listen," she would whisper to me. "They're getting hungry." She would approach the bureau and then make a big deal of carefully extracting them so that she wouldn't get bitten. I could run but I couldn't hide and it was even worse when I tried because then I had those beady little eyes glinting at me in dark places.

Her resentment partially stemmed from the fact that she was forced to baby-sit my brother and me from an early age, when she could have been out with her friends, or later, baby-sitting other people's kids for money. I have no memory of her reading us a book, playing a board game or even feeding us while she was in charge.

She left home when she was seventeen, and I was ten. Her marriage was a hurried affair — more anger and shouting and blame. Her romantic escape to freedom led her into even harder circumstances. Her first home had neither electricity nor indoor plumbing, except for a hand pump for water in the kitchen sink. She had her first three children in three years and then another three after a short hiatus.

I was called on to pinch-hit for her once when she had to leave her small community to have all her teeth extracted and false teeth fitted. The long-term effect of no childhood dental care and poor dental advice during years of nearly constant pregnancy had left her no other options. Before the age of her majority, she was left toothless.

Defanged, she might have been, but you would be mistaken if you were to think it rendered her harmless.

She got her family out of the backwash they were moldering in by convincing her much older husband that their fortune was to be found on Vancouver Island, not in the interior of B.C. And that is where I found them after I left home to attend university.

But her family circumstances seemed even more bleak to me when I paid my first visit. Huge cedars dripped non-stop from above the little house they occupied. The yard was a quagmire and the sour, dank odour emanating from the bathroom was the smell I came to associate with that place. There was even a huge hole in the floor of the kids' bedroom that left the squalid little room exposed to the damp earth below. My heart ached for those children. How could parents leave it like that? A piece of plywood would have covered it up and made the room so much safer and more habitable. Money for cigarettes and endless pots of coffee but not a cent for home improvement, I observed.

Her approach to childcare was so inconsistent her kids were totally confused:

"Jimmy, put down the knife, you'll hurt someone."

"Jimmy, I said bring me the knife."

"Jimmy, if you don't stop poking that knife at your sister, I am going to wring your bloody neck."

But she never moved a muscle, and Jimmy carried on with impunity, eventually throwing the knife down in boredom and finding something else to make his sister's life miserable.

Then his sister walked over to stand beside her mother, and as she swung around to cuddle in, her hand caught the coffee cup her mother was about to drink from, and all hell broke loose. A bit of spilled coffee rated a major spanking and raging verbal abuse that culminated in a frightened four-year-old being dragged, kicking and screaming, to her room.

My face must have registered my distress because it was on this visit that Bernice began to manifest a new attitude toward me.

"You know you were always Dad's favourite," she informed me in an after dinner discussion that quickly turned into a guilt trip. "From the time you were born, it was Janice this and Janice that. You could 'sing like a nightingale, read before you started school, carry on an adult conversation at four, draw, paint and create anything you put your hand to,'" she intoned in an imitation of our father's voice. "It was sickening the way he carried on," she complained.

"But you could play the piano, and you did well at school," I said, trying to placate.

Bernice rolled her eyes. "That didn't count, as far as he was concerned. What did you get for your sixteenth birthday?"

"I think I got a small am radio for my bedroom," I recalled.

"And what did I get? Nothing!"

"But you had already quit school and had a job when you were sixteen. You were no longer even speaking to Mom and Dad because you wanted to get married and they were against it. And besides that, by then, Bob was buying you all kinds of gifts. I remember . . ."

"That has nothing to do with it. And speaking of school, who was the only one to finish school — of all us kids — and go on to university? You! I know they wouldn't have done a thing to help me get there."

"Well, as a matter of fact, they never did much to help me either. I had to get loans and bursaries. You know where all their disposable income went. Straight to the bar."

"How can you talk about them that way when they gave you everything?" Bernice railed.

And so it went. I never made a return visit until after I was married. My husband and I moved to Victoria, a few miles from her family.

"Well it certainly took you long enough to get here," Bernice snarked. "Ashamed to bring your new husband around?"

That was closer to the mark than I wanted to admit. "May I point out that the road is the same distance both ways," I replied. But in five years of living in the same city, she only visited me once.

Around the time that my husband and I were about to leave Victoria, my parents were starting to experience health problems that were exacerbated by their living conditions. Their old, uninsulated house would freeze up in the winter and my mother would have to carry water from a neighbour's place for weeks on end. The place was falling apart, and it was pretty clear to me that they would have to find other quarters as they grew older and less able to cope.

My husband and I had discussed the possibility of sharing the financial burden of building them a small house amongst all four siblings. I edged toward that suggestion when the topic of our parents came up on our last visit to my sister and her family before we moved from Victoria.

"What do you mean?" asked Bernice.

"I just thought since things are getting so hard for them as they get older, maybe we could all pitch in and build them a smaller place on their property."

"What did they ever do for me," Bernice began. "Mom wouldn't even tear herself away to come and help when I had hepatitis with five little kids to look after and two still in diapers."

"Gee," I said, "that must have been at least twelve years ago. Don't you think it's time to forgive and forget?"

"Some things I'll never forget," she vowed.

"So I guess you are not interested in contributing to the project?"

"No bloody way. I have more important things to spend my money on. We're not all high-paid teachers you know,"

And didn't I know it! But her husband, Bob, also a peacemaker, born between the two great wars, said, "Come on, honey, play the piano for us. These guys haven't heard you play on the honky-tonk piano, and you've been practicing all those old ragtime tunes."

So we moved to the living room, and my sister kept us entertained for the next two hours with ragtime, boogie-woogie, country, standards, Broadway hits and pop tunes. If she could hear it, she could play it, instinctively knowing which chords to use and how to change from one genre to another. However, that night everything reverberated because of the tacks she had stuck into the felt hammers of the piano. Animosity and bad feelings were swept away in a wave of continuous music: we called out the songs and she met the challenge. She was happy! For hours she laughed and played, escaping her difficult life by entering the world of song.

Several nights later Bernice telephoned.

"I know what you're planning," she said.

"Planning?" I asked.

"You're trying to steal my birthright," she accused.

"You have a birthright?" I asked.

"You know what I mean. That old house and property were left to Dad by Grandma to hand down to us when he died. You are trying to get your hands on it, and I won't stand by and let you do it."

"But you didn't want to have anything to do with building a house for them, so the rest of us kids thought we would see what we could do."

"I am not going to be robbed of my inheritance. If I have to get a second mortgage on this place, I will, before I'll see you run off with everything."

"So you are in on the project now?"

"You're damn right I am!"

We never reconciled after that. I ceased making the effort to visit her and the road was always too long to my place, I guess.

She's gone now. I picture her as a Valkyrie, riding across Valhalla with horns and a spear, stirring things up in the firmament and not taking any guff from anyone. I expect Odin's life is a little harder now.

Older than Barbie

By Jody Chadderton

Not exactly "breaking news" but a news item just the same: Mattel's Barbie is turning 50! Who cares? you might ask. You're right, I don't really care about Barbie anymore either, except it came as a shock to find out that, at fifty-one and a half, I am older than Barbie. How did that happen?

Several decades of grown-up girls like myself still remember their very first Barbie doll. I got mine when I was 6 or 7. She was long-legged and curvy with painted-on makeup and feet permanently bent into a tippy-toe position for her high-heeled shoes. My Barbie had auburn hair parted on the side and swept into a long side pony tail. She was beautiful.

After I got my Barbie, I had to have all the Barbie accessories. I got a shiny black suitcase for all her clothes and, over the years, more than enough clothes to fill it. Mom sewed and knit Barbie clothes for my sisters and me. One year for Christmas Mom used toothpicks to knit a lemon yellow turtleneck ski sweater for my Barbie. Problem was, I had to pull Barbie's head off in order to get the sweater on. Also, the cuffs were too tight for the hands to fit through, so I pretended that it was a very special sweater with built-in mittens. When Mom sewed pedal-pushers and a pop top for me the next summer, my Barbie got one to match. Barbie's actually outlasted mine. I fell down and skinned my knee and ruined my pedal pushers long before I had a chance to outgrow them.

We made our own Barbie house out of the old console record player which no longer worked. Dad took the old turntable and radio out so we had lots of room for Barbie furniture. Kate, a friend of my sister's, showed us how to make beds and upholstered chairs using lint from the dryer for stuffing. We cut berry baskets to look like lawn furniture, and small boxes could be used as tables. My Barbie had a boyfriend who I called Don after my dad. I still thought my dad was the most handsome man I knew. The Don doll wasn't a Ken anyway but a generic knock-off. He had his own red convertible, but he couldn't sit in it properly because his knees didn't bend. My friend Janice had horses for her Barbie. When I took my Barbie to Janice's, she let me pretend that my Barbie had her very own horse.

No one else we knew had the Barbie board game that we had. Friends and cousins always asked to play the Barbie game when they came to visit. To win, you needed to obtain a boyfriend, a prom dress and a car in order to make it to the prom. Of course, we all wanted Ken, the black strapless number and the red roadster, but eventually we each realized that the important thing was to get all three components and win. Just like in real life (although we probably didn't know it then) it was easier to get beady-eyed, freckly Poindexter, the beater and the beige dress.

When I was a kid, Barbie was either a teenager or a young adult. In other words, she was a good 10 years or more older than I. So if I'm 50-something, Barbie would be in her 60's, right? Only she's not. Barbie was born a teenager or a 20-something depending on which version you look at. You see, Cheerleader Barbie or Roller Skate Barbie was probably a school girl, while Doctor Barbie or Teacher Barbie was a young adult. Barbie was never a baby or even a child. So, she was born full-grown while I was a very small child, and she stayed pretty much the same age — give or take a few, depending on what she was depicted doing or being on a particular day — until now. Now, all of a sudden, she's turning 50.

Well, she's not really. She still looks perky and cute and cheerleader-y. Still like a teen or twenty-something. And I am not. I look into my magic mirror, and I see myself as youthful and slender. But when the magic fails, I see the wrinkles and lumps, evidence of years of gravity and some real-life fun times taking their toll.   I don't want to be a teenager or even in my twenties again. I really don't. I am happy for the life experience that has greyed my hair and lined my skin. But I don't want to be older than Barbie. It just doesn't seem fair.

A Moment's Hesitation

By Allene Halliday

Why did I turn to stone
unable to speak or move?
My hero was so close
I could have whispered;
he would have heard me.
I could have reached out
and easily touched him.

He gazed at me expectantly.
I remained frozen in place;
the paralysis unconquered.
And so the moment passed.
Helpless, I watched him disappear.
He will never know
what I longed to tell him.

It wasn't raining,
he wasn't singing,
and he wasn't dancing.
But it was Beverley Hills
at Camden and Little Santa Monica.

The Sheep Shearing

By Anita L. Trapler

During the back-to-the-land movement and those days of self-actualization, my husband and I, who wore city skins through and through, tried on the country life for size.

We hadn't been in the business of raising sheep for long, having purchased two pregnant Suffolk ewes in late fall. Then we added a speckle-faced Suffolk-Cheviot cross, a Cheviot, and a black-faced, rangy ewe to which no one could attach a lineage. We were attracted to this old sheep because she lacked grace and proportion. She was ugly. But, she was the mother of a scrubby, irresistible charcoal ram lamb.

The farmer, from whom we purchased the ram and its mother, described unrestrained sheep as "jumping beans." He quickly popped the lamb into a potato sack, fastened the end, then set the animal on the floor of the cab of our half-ton truck.

The sacked lamb wrestled around, poked its head out of the tied end of the potato sack and scrambled to its feet, keenly alert and curious about whatever was happening. The little ram resembled a child's stuffed toy, which you simply wanted to pick up and hug.

Whenever we transported small livestock, I rode in the back of the pick-up to shield and comfort the little beasties. I ensured that we all safely arrived at our destination. So this time, too, I rode in the back of the truck and straddled the frightened mother, just in case she loosened the foot bindings and attempted a hasty departure over the side.

None the worse for their journey, the two animals joined the other grazing sheep in our friend, Patrick's grassy pasture in Alderley. All our livestock were housed and pastured at our friend's acreage.

We soon discovered that sheep are truly bashful, awkward, completely silly animals, whose fleecy coats must be sheared once a year.

I enthusiastically volunteered for the job. If First Nations women could shear sheep, card wool and weave blankets, I figured I too, could shear sheep. Or, so I thought.

I'd seen sheep shearing done on the television drama, *The Thorn Birds*. The sheep seemed tractable and easy to manage. Most of the animals quietly waited or simply lay around while the shearers rapidly stripped one animal after another of their fleece.

As the weather grew warmer in May, my nervous husband said, "Soon, we'll have to shear the sheep."

"I'll shear them," I promised, again, "if you hang on to them." But with the swift passage of time, my confidence seeped out like air from an over-inflated tire. In our home library we had several *Harrowsmith* magazines and a number of self-sufficiency books. However, none of these books really described sheep shearing in an instructive way, only that the act of sheep shearing is a matter of stripping the fleece in one entire piece and the sheep don't like it one bit.

A magazine article advised that when one purchases any ewe, she should first be examined for having both "mammaries" intact. A careless shearer can accidentally cut off a nipple. It's rather like a barber or hairdresser accidentally removing a slice of a patron's ear along with the hair.

After studying the situation more closely, I could see I was out of my league. We decided to call an experienced sheep shearer. One who had served a rigorous apprenticeship.

The weather grew warmer; the ewes more "pant-y."

We were really uneasy. Wilf had horrible visions of the ewes wearing their woolly coats the entire summer, and by the last week in May, he was getting desperate.

Over a cup of coffee on the sundeck, he threatened, "I'll have to come up with a sheep shearer, or those ladies are off to the abattoir. Far better to put them down than let them suffer in this heat."

"No, no, no!" I shrieked. "I can't bear to see our ladies hanging upside down in some cooler. Even if they are too hot right now."

Trying to defuse the situation, I offered, "The ewes are surrounded by a wire fence, maybe they'll catch some of their wool and unravel themselves." It was a cartoon I had seen. Even under the most difficult of circumstances, a sense of humour ought to prevail. But my husband shot me one of these withering glances which suggested I ought to say no more. And for the time being I held my peace.

"I'll give it one more week," he said. "Either we find a shearer, or Madame T., the Suffolk-Cheviot cross, Tu-Tu Six Too, that shabby, rangy ewe and the rest of them are mutton." He slammed his coffee cup on the table. "No stone will be left unturned. I will find a sheep shearer!"

This was no exaggeration. To secure what he's after, my husband would overturn every pebble on a beach.

Wilf sent frantic signals to several sources in the community which had contact with sheep shearers. Early one evening, I received a phone call from an excited Patrick saying that a sheep shearer had arrived. My over-worked husband was already at Patrick's, cultivating corn so I said I would join them. The shearing was about to begin.

I collected an extension cord, iodine, a hoof trimming knife, Wonder Dust Rotenone, which is a flea and tick powder, and a pair of leather gloves. Just as I arrived, a tall, blond youth was helping Wilf carry an upside down reluctant Cheviot to the back of the truck. They heaved her in. All five "ladies" had to be gathered together at the top of the field, nearest to an electrical outlet. We had not mastered the art of draping a sheep over our shoulders as the shepherds of yore had done.

216

In paintings, pastoral poetry and in photographs, sheep are shown as calm, gentle, unruffled animals. They are, up until the time you want them to do something. Then they become as skittish as rabbits, and flighty as chickens.

In any event, I rode in the back of the truck, draped around an extremely hot ewe. The truck bounced in the rutted dirt road, a few hundred feet to the top of the pasture.

I became aware of a thick, rancid odour and the ewe's woolly coat felt greasy. There was smooth oil, mixed with sweat, on the palms of my hands. So this is the oil used in various ointments. The odour is neutralized and the oil becomes lanolin. Somehow, I couldn't imagine anyone smearing that smelly brown mixture anywhere.

My husband braked the truck, leapt out and scurried around to one of the chicken houses looking for an outlet for the extension cord. Peter, the sheep shearer, was self-assured and in complete control. He casually strolled over to the sheep shed to prepare his equipment. Four curious ewes followed him. Meanwhile I remained in the back of the truck restraining and comforting the bug-eyed Cheviot. I was becoming over-heated. I began to feel like I was nestled against a really hot stove.

I felt abandoned. The Cheviot was silent. I screamed, "Get me out of here!"

Relief finally came, as the shearer and Wilf lifted the rumpled ewe off the truck and guided her through the gate. I hoisted myself off the back of the truck, dripping sweat, exhausted and grumpy. Naturally, I was ignored. It was the other "ladies" who were the centre of all the attention.

My husband loped off for a can of oats to lure all five ewes into the sheepfold.

Sheep will follow, but they are the most difficult animals to herd anywhere, individually and collectively becoming the most obstinate and contrary of creatures.

Eventually, all five animals were confined. The first sheep selected was "Mrs. T." The shearer managed to manoeuvre the ewe over to a plywood board under the electric shears. He up-ended the ewe and seated the animal on her rump.

When positioned in this ridiculously undignified manner, the animal was amazingly amenable to handling. With the shear switched on, Peter whipped it down the ewe's throat and along the underline, deftly trimming the foreleg and removing the underbelly wool. With not a sigh or a bleat from Mrs. T., her woolly coat was peeled off, a little like a banana skin, in scarcely over a minute. When the shearling's woolly coat was removed, she didn't appear any larger than a rather ample dog. Her pink hide gleamed in the shadows of the sheepfold. The other four sheep stood in a corner of the shed and watched in wary fascination. Mrs. T., powdered and trimmed, gambolled about like a baby lamb in "sheer" ecstasy. All five ewes were naked in less than half an hour.

We named our now exposed, well-endowed little ram, "Biggy." We had reason to hope for a nice crop of lambs from his efforts, but he didn't like the shearing anymore than the rest of them did.

As suddenly as the shearer had shown up, his work came to an end. We were effusive in our praise and gratitude. No wonder in days past there were feasts and celebrations after a sheep shearing event.

For the three of us, a nice cold beer sufficed.

Where the Heart Is

By Sue Whittaker

Where twilight bathes the evening hills
in softest lavender and rose,
there is where the heart is,
there is where it goes.

Where wood smoke drifts from orchard fires
rising over Kobau's crests,
there is where the heart is,
there is where it rests.

And does the bridge still beckon
to youths, in early spring?
Calling for that leap of faith,
the annual christening?

Do spicy apple blossoms scent
the air through April nights?
Do vineyards glow with velvet fuzz?
Do children run with kites?

How I long to be there,
joining in the fun.
Planting pansies, turning soil,
worshipping the sun.

Contributors

Sheila Blimke

After raising a family in lovely, vibrant Alberta, Sheila and her husband retired from public service with the Federal Government and built their retirement home in beautiful Osoyoos, BC. Sheila says, "Surrounded by sparkling lakes, mountains, vineyards and orchards, we find it a retiree's paradise."

In *Whispering Down the Well,* Sheila recounts the stories of several amazing women from her ancestry.

With women such as these as role models it is no surprise that Sheila was imbued with courage, a positive outlook and a wry sense of humour.

Jody Chadderton

Jody's joint passions for reading and writing led her to pursue a B.A. in English from Simon Fraser University. While there, she had her first experience with a writing club. The experience was positive, but the club petered out after the first summer. Jody continued to write poems and short prose pieces and was thrilled to be part of O's Own Writers from the start.

A native of B.C., Jody moved to Osoyoos with her husband in 1993 and is happy to say this is home.

Allene Halliday

Allene Halliday is a transplanted Californian who "discovered" the beautiful Okanagan several years ago. She now lives "south of the border" in Oroville, Washington. Her hobbies include gardening, singing, dancing, visiting grandchildren and occasionally acting in local amateur theatre productions. Allene is becoming well-known for her one woman shows that bring back the glory days of Vaudeville theatre.

She has contributed some beautiful vignettes to *Whispering Down the Well*, personal experiences that might well have been lost had she not retrieved them from her memory and shared them with her fellow writers and you, the reader.

Maureen Kresfelder

Maureen was born and raised in Vancouver. Her desire to see more of the world inspired her to backpack in Europe for a year and teach in Nigeria for 3 years. She also spent 25 years teaching in BC. She is married to Lionel and has 3 step-children. She states, "In retirement I have discovered writing. It has become a marvelous way of interpreting, describing and illuminating my life — even when I write fiction."

Everett Marwood

Author of *A Legacy Worth Leaving – savoring the past, inspiring the future*   Trafford 2003

Everett Marwood is thrilled to be welcomed as a part of the O's Own Writers. For 14 years he has shared his life between Calgary, AB and Osoyoos, BC, enjoying the lifestyles of the two regions. Everett also has fond memories of living in the provinces of Quebec and Ontario and has relished the opportunities to

222

travel to all the regions of this country and many other parts of the world.

Everett says, "I treasure the relationships developed with the contributing authors of *Whispering Down the Well* and I hope all readers enjoy the sentiments shared through the stories and poems by these wonderful authors."

Maureen Olson

Maureen Olson has spent 18 productive and stimulating years in Osoyoos. She feels that joining the O's Own writing group was a pivotal move. "What a supportive, creative and caring group of developing writers," she states.

Maureen would like to thank the Osoyoos and District Arts Council for their grant-in-aid that supported O's Own in securing workshops through OUC to strengthen writing skills and encourage experimentation.

"I am amazed with the talents we now have and look forward to continued growth. And new members are always welcome and add stimulation," she reminds everyone.

Sally Swedberg

Sally was born in Des Moines, Iowa, and the United States was her home until she met her husband in 1955.

"He was from Minnesota but taking his seminary schooling in Canada. We were married in 1956 and since then, have lived mostly in Canada and enjoy dual citizenship."

Sally has been writing poetry, articles and short stories for many years and has had several articles and a short story published.

"Living in Liberia, West Africa for seven years, visiting Haiti two times and now retired in Osoyoos since 1998 has given me lots to write about," says Sally.

Anita Trapler

Anita Trapler moved from Osoyoos to Victoria in 2008 but still remains a part of the O's Own Writers. She has always been interested in the Arts so joining O's Own was a natural step for her.

While participating in the OUC writing workshops that paved the way for this collection of writing, Anita was able to polish several stories she had been developing over time and bring to life the story of her remarkable mother-in-law, Antonia, a story that would otherwise have been "whispered down the well" and lost to memory.

Because of modern lines of communication, the other members of O's Own are pleased to be able to keep in touch with Anita in her new environs and delight in her letters and phone calls.

Sue Whittaker

Sue Whittaker comes from a long line of women who throughout their lives overcame desperate situations including emigration, the Great Depression, two World Wars, and for a few, lamentable choices of husbands.

The stories from Sue's husband's family were equally daunting although the husbands, in those cases, were comparative princes.

With this story material resonating within her, Sue shouldered the challenge to retrieve stories from the well and create a few others that reflect her incurable romanticism.

Her poems, she says, are brief insights that just happened along the way.